A Pennyworth of Peppermints

A Pennyworth of Peppermints

A story set in the First World War

Mary Weeks Millard

Dernier Publishing

First published 2014
Published by Dernier Publishing
P.O. Box 793, Orpington, BR6 1FA, England
www.dernierpublishing.com

ISBN 9780956904331

Production services by RoperPenberthy Publishing Ltd

For my grandchildren, Jade, Danielle, Louise, Jason and Lisa, to help you remember your great-great-great-uncle Joe White, who fought bravely for his country in the Great War of 1914–1918.

Acknowledgements

I would like to say thank you to Janet Wilson of Dernier Publishing for all her help and encouragement. Also, thanks to my ever patient husband, Malcolm, for all the help he has given. My thanks also to the librarian at Littlemoor Library, Weymouth, for helping me in the research for this book. Finally, my thanks to Jean Howell, for telling me the story of her father's experiences in the First World War, and allowing me to see his documents.

Author's Note

Although the places mentioned in this book are all real places in Dorset, the story and all the characters are entirely imaginary.

All asterisked words and phrases* are explained in the Glossary at the back of the book.

Chapter One

"Hello, Ben. Now let me guess. Would you be wanting a pennyworth of peppermints this morning, by any chance?" asked the shopkeeper, Mr. Savage. Mr. Savage's name was all wrong, Ben thought to himself. He's kind and friendly and always gentle! But then, my name's a funny one, too. Fancy being called "Goodenough"!

"Yes please, Mr. Savage," answered Ben, as he handed over four farthings*. He watched the shopkeeper weigh out the peppermints in his large shiny, brass scale and then put them into a twist of paper.

"Thank you," said Ben, as he put the sweets in his pocket. Every Saturday he took his pocket money to the shop and bought his peppermints. They were his favourite type of sweets and he chose them every week. Sometimes Mr. Savage popped in an extra sweet or two for his regular ten-year-old customer.

"So what's the news in your house?" Mr. Savage asked. "Have you heard from Fred this week?" Fred was Ben's big brother and was a soldier in the Dorsetshire Regiment*, fighting in France.

"No news from Fred, but today is Albert's birthday. Now he is seventeen he's going to enlist* in the army, too. Our mum's really upset about it; she wanted him to finish his apprenticeship with the blacksmith. He says he's not going to let anyone give him a white feather* for being a coward. He wants to join the army. Mum doesn't know how she's going to manage without his wages, though. His wages are more than the allowance the army gives to soldiers. She is thinking she'll ask for a job in the munitions factory, but Dad is dead against it. He says it'll turn her yellow!"

"Yes, some of my customers who work there making ammunition for the guns certainly have problems with their skin and hair turning a funny colour – but not everyone. It's hard times we live in son! This war* has been on for two years already and there seems no hope of it ending soon. I'll tell you what, though, since it's Albert's birthday, I'll give you a packet of Marie biscuits. Bit of a treat for you all!"

"Cor, thanks Mr. Savage," said Ben, his face lighting up. He said goodbye and ran all the way home through the village of Chickerell to the tiny old cottage in the nearby small village of Charlestown, where he lived.

The cottage was down a lane, near the lagoon called The Fleet, which nestled behind the huge Chesil beach. The locals called the lagoon "Littlesea", and Ben's dad was a fisherman who worked both in Littlesea and around Portland. The lane was just a muddy cart track, and Ben's cottage was the only house in it. It was a very old building, with a thatched roof where lots of spiders lived, and which leaked when it rained heavily.

There was a small front garden where Ben's mother liked to grow flowers, and a narrow path that led to the front door. Downstairs there were two main rooms. First there was the kitchen, where everyone spent most of their time. This had a small scullery* and a larder* leading off it, and then there was a nice sitting room, which the family used on Sundays and special occasions.

Upstairs there were two bedrooms; one where Ben's parents slept and the other that he shared with Albert. It was a simple home, but the family had always been happy there. Upstairs there were wooden floorboards, but no carpets. Ben's mum had made rag rugs from old sacks with pieces of cloth pushed through them, to make it a little warmer when they got out of bed. Downstairs there were tiles on the floor, laid over packed-down mud. When it was very wet worms sometimes came up through the cracks! Behind the door into the sitting room was a heavy curtain on a brass pole to help keep out the draught. In the kitchen, the stove helped to keep them warm in the winter.

"Guess what Mum?" Ben asked as he burst into the little cottage. "Mr. Savage has given us a packet of biscuits to celebrate Albert's birthday!"

"My goodness, what a kind man he is – and what a treat!" said his Mum, her face lighting up with a smile. "I was wondering what to do to make it a special day. Molly's having her half day today, too, instead of tomorrow."

Molly was Ben's sister, who was in service* at the manor house in the nearby village of Radipole. She was eighteen, and hated being a servant, even though her employer, Lady Worthington, was a very kind person. Molly had dreams of doing something exciting with her life, rather than just cleaning, preparing vegetables and clearing up after meals! She lived in the "Big House", as Radipole Manor was fondly called by the local people, sharing a bedroom in the attic with the cook, and only coming home on her half day each week.

"Do you need me now, Mum?" Ben asked. "I said to Sidney that I'd go with him and look for driftwood for the stove*."

"I'll make you a sandwich," said his mum, cutting two thick slices of bread and spreading them with margarine and sprinkling them with a tiny bit of sugar for a treat. "Take a sack and see what you can find, but be back by four."

With his sandwich in one hand and the sack in the other, Ben whistled as he walked up the lane and along the road to the neighbouring village of Wyke Regis. His school friend, Sidney, lived there. He came from a big family and had ten brothers and sisters. Ben got most of their names muddled up except for Vera, who was Sid's twin sister, and who looked very much like him.

Sid was waiting for him and when he saw Ben he quickly fetched his sack and the two of them set off for Chesil beach. "Race you to the sea!" shouted Sid, as soon as they reached the beach. They scrambled down the steep bank of pebbles and arrived at the seashore, breathless and laughing.

Ben loved it here: the smell of the salty seaweed, the gentle rhythm of the waves and the vast expanse of sea. He pulled his bag of peppermints from his pocket and offered one to his friend. The boys sucked them noisily as they started to look for pieces of wood that had been washed up on the shore. It was a rare treat for Sidney to have a sweet. With so many children in his family he didn't get any pocket money, even though he had to work very hard helping out at home.

The previous week had been stormy, which was unusual for May. This meant that a lot of wood had been washed up on the shore. Once their sacks were full, the boys sat on the pebbles and Ben shared his sandwich with Sid. It was warm and sunny, so they decided to have a paddle. They knew there were only a few safe places to swim along this part of the coastline, so they contented themselves with staying near the shore and kicking the water at each other.

Sometimes when they were on the beach they would watch the fishermen taking their boats out or mending their nets on the shore. Ben saw his dad and grandad from time to time, working with their mates in the lerrets*, but they were nowhere to be seen that afternoon.

"Hey!" cried Sidney, suddenly. He bent down in the water and at first Ben thought that a crab must have pinched him. Instead, his friend pulled up a glass bottle. "Wow! There's something inside it – a piece of paper!" Sidney exclaimed. "I wonder what it says!"

Chapter Two

The two boys climbed back on to the bank of pebbles carrying the bottle. It had a glass stopper and something like sealing wax over the top.

"It must have been sealed to stop any water getting in and spoiling the message," said Ben. "I think we should take it home to open it. We don't want to leave broken glass on the beach."

"You're right," agreed Sid. "You'd better take it to your house. There are too many little 'uns at ours: someone would spoil it or tear up the message … it might even get used as loo paper! There isn't anywhere I can hide anything safely."

Sometimes Ben felt sorry for Sid. Everything was a terrible squeeze at his house. The children slept four to a bed, two one end and two the other. There was hardly anywhere in the house Sid could be on his own. "Anyway, I'd better be going," said Sid. "Don't open the bottle without me, will you?"

Ben pulled a face. "Not sure I can wait that long!" he said. "Only joking," he added as he saw Sidney looking disappointed. "Fancy another peppermint?"

"Thanks," replied his friend, as they picked up their

sacks of driftwood and started walking back to Sid's house together. It was always much harder to walk up the pebble bank than to run down it, especially with their heavy load of driftwood! The boys decided to meet after Sunday School the next day and then they would try to open the bottle.

On the way they passed the workers coming out from Whitehead Torpedo Works*, at the end of their shift. Ben thought they looked worn out. They might not be soldiers, but to the boys they were still heroes, making torpedoes to blow up enemy ships. Sid spotted his dad and ran over to him, calling goodbye to Ben.

It was quite a long walk for Ben after that, but he had a lot to think about. He thought about his brother enlisting and what it would be like to go off and fight for your country. He thought about Sid having no room to stretch his legs in bed. He thought about his mum working in a factory that could make you ill. And he wondered what message he and Sid would discover in the bottle tomorrow. His stomach rumbled noisily, as it often did these days. He was looking forward to Albert's special birthday tea!

"There you are!" said Molly, as soon as he entered the cottage, running over to him and giving him a quick hug. Ben was pleased to see his sister. She always wanted to know what he had been doing and how things had been at school, even though she was so much older than him. She took the sack of driftwood. "Look mum, our Ben has a whole sack of wood! Shall I put it outside to dry?"

"Well done, Ben," said Albert. "I know you'll help mum when I'm gone. Just fancy, you'll have a whole bedroom to yourself while I'm away! Mind you, don't take over. I shall be back and so will our Fred as soon as this war is finished. We'll beat those Huns*!"

The family had tea as soon as Dad came in. It was a wonderful tea, almost like the days before the war*. Their mother had made sandwiches with real butter and meat paste. She had opened a jar of her home-made chutney, too. There was half a boiled egg for each of them and she had spread a thin layer of jam between two Marie biscuits, making them like cakes. It was delicious!

"I'm signing on, on Monday," Albert announced. "I want to be in the new tank regiment. So long as I pass the medical I'll be trained at Bovington camp. That's only the other side of Dorchester, so I won't be very far away. These new machines will win the war for us and I will be part of it! Then I'll be sent to fight at the front line* where the battle is really happening, but we'll be safe inside those tanks. They're amazing machines. I'm convinced they will win the war for us."

"Why are they called 'tanks'?" Ben asked.

"It's to trick the enemy into thinking they are just water tanks, but really they are weapons which can cross the trenches. They are so thick that men are safe inside them," Albert answered.

"What are the trenches?" Ben asked his brother, "Everyone talks about being in the trenches."

"At the front line, the men dig deep channels or trenches, where they can be hidden from enemy sight. These trenches are often very muddy and cold and horrible to live in. That's why women like Mum knit the soldiers thick socks, to try and keep their feet dry. If the soldiers' feet stay wet they can get 'trench foot', and their feet are rotten and very painful. When the soldiers fight, they have to climb up out of the trench and run at the enemy. It's called 'going over the top'," explained Albert.

"I tell you what," suggested Molly, "when you leave to go to the front, we'll try to come and see you off at Weymouth railway station, or maybe even at London, won't we Ben?"

"That would be great! I could even get a day off school for that!"

"Maybe you could," said Dad, and smiled at Molly, "and perhaps they will give you a day off work, too. You work so hard over there." Ben could see that his Mum and Dad didn't want to make a fuss at the birthday tea about Albert going away, but he noticed a sad look pass between them.

It was so nice having a birthday tea with all the family that Ben forgot about the bottle until later that evening. Then, when he remembered, he wondered if he should tell Albert. He decided against it, because he didn't want his brother insisting on opening it without Sid. He wanted to keep his promise. So he hid the bottle under his bed where no one would find it, and fell asleep dreaming about secret messages.

Sunday was always a busy day for everyone. In the war years almost everyone in England went to church and the children were sent to Sunday School in the afternoon. It was the one day of the week when Ben's dad didn't take out the lerret. Instead, he dressed in his best clothes and took all the family to Chickerell church, as there wasn't one in Charlestown. These days, Ben had a sense of dread as he walked to church. Some weeks the minister read out the list of those from the parish who had died at war or were reported missing or injured. Some of them were young men whom Ben had known when they were schoolboys. A few had even lied about their ages and joined up when they were only fourteen or fifteen. Fortunately, this Sunday there were no names read out, and everyone sighed with relief and thanked God for his mercy.

In his sermon the minister said that everyone needed to fight, not against the Germans, but against the evil in the world, and all the work of Satan. Ben felt a bit confused by that. Wasn't this whole war about fighting the Germans? Didn't everyone hate them?

Sunday School was held in the village hall. It was packed with children and Sidney was there with all his younger brothers and sisters. Sometimes Ben envied him. He wished he had some brothers or sisters nearer his age. One day, when he was about seven years old he had overheard the butcher's wife telling someone that he was an "accident", because he had arrived so long after his older brothers and sister. It had made him feel very sad and as if he wasn't really wanted. Perhaps his mum and dad had felt like they had all the family they wanted and then he arrived and upset it all. Although he loved his parents very much and felt that they loved him, there was always this sadness at the back of his mind, even though he tried to push it away.

Ben, Sidney and Vera always sat together. Once they had settled, Ben quietly slipped a peppermint to each of his friends. He knew they had so little to eat in their house that they were often hungry. Some days they just had bread to eat with a cup of tea. Both children smiled in appreciation.

The story seemed to go on for ever that afternoon. Usually Ben loved the exciting Bible stories of heroes like David who killed the giant, and Daniel who survived being thrown into a den of hungry lions, but today all he could think about was the bottle and the message.

As soon as Sunday School was over he asked Sid if he could come and open the bottle. "Can our Vera come, too?" he asked, "She's always having to look after the babies, but it would be fun for her."

Ben hesitated. He wasn't sure he wanted a girl around. She might spoil things. But he didn't want to look mean. "Yes, of course. Come as soon as you can. Mum will give you some tea, I'm sure."

"That would be great. We'll run home with the little ones and then come," said Sid. Vera looked so happy at being included that Ben felt ashamed he'd not wanted her to come. He was glad he'd said yes, after all.

An hour later the twins arrived at the cottage. Ben's mother knew that Sidney and Vera's parents struggled to feed their large family, so she had produced another really lovely tea, as much as she could manage, including the remains of the Marie biscuits. The children ate hungrily.

After tea, Ben, Sid and Vera went outside to the bottom of the back garden. They took the bottle with them, and a brick to break it open. Ben had found an old sack. He thought if they broke the bottle over the sack they could collect up all the glass and nobody would get hurt. They were all so excited when Ben carefully pulled out the message.

"You read it Vera," said Ben, handing her the piece of paper. "You're the best reader in our class at school."

The writing was a bit faint, but written in a beautiful copperplate* hand.

Whoever finds this, rich or poor,
Washed up, I hope, upon the shore;
Near a fleet where no fleet can sail,
Near a port from whence the plague did hail
There is a village which rhymes with hole
And in the churchyard, beware, a mole!
Catch him, and help to win the war.
Find his tunnel with a hidden store,
But he is cunning – so beware!
And for your life, please take care.

And there's another thing I say,
My name is Captain Arthur Wray.
Tell my wife I love her dear;
Tell my wife to have no fear
For I shall wake on another shore
To be with Jesus for evermore.

"Oh! It's just a silly rhyme, it doesn't make sense," said Sidney, screwing up his face in disappointment.

"No Sid," said Vera. "It *is* a poem, but it has some sort of hidden meaning."

"That's right," answered Ben, getting very excited. "It's a mystery poem, full of clues which we have to work out. We have to be detectives!"

Just then the church clock struck the hour. "Bother, we'll have to go now," Sidney said with a sigh. "We'll have to discuss it tomorrow, we mustn't be late back. Mum needs us to help get the young 'uns to bed. Keep the message safe and we'll see you tomorrow in school."

Chapter Three

After Sidney and Vera had gone home Ben sat on the garden wall, thinking about the message in the bottle. He was sure it was a real mystery to solve! The first clue was very easy for him to work out. It had to mean the Fleet or Littlesea where they lived. No fleet of ships could sail in the Fleet; it was too small and too shallow.

He vaguely remembered hearing that the great plague had begun because rats had escaped off a boat. Could it have been Weymouth or Lyme Regis or West Bay? He was still pondering this when his brother, Albert, came to find him.

"Ben, now that I am going into the army, I ought to teach you how to catch rabbits*. You know how often mum has been glad to have the extra meat! I'm going to give you my catapult. It's still light, so we'll go to the fields just by the Fleet and see what we can do."

Ben jumped off the wall. "I'd love to learn. Can I really have your catapult?"

As the brothers walked together from the cottage down the lane to the fields, Albert explained a bit more about catching rabbits.

"You find a place near their burrows and sit quietly.

You need a few small round pebbles from the beach. Have a stone ready in the catapult so that when the rabbit comes out of the burrow you can sling the stone. Usually the rabbit pauses before he hops off and that is the moment to try. Aim for the head; usually the stone knocks the rabbit out or kills it outright. I keep my penknife handy. If it is just unconscious I can kill it instantly. There are thousands of rabbits in this field, but I never take more than two or three. Just take what you need for the pot."

Ben was excited, but also a bit scared. He didn't like the idea of killing anything but he knew he had to be brave. He sat beside Albert, not even daring to move lest he make a noise and scare off the rabbits. They were popping in and out of their burrows all the time. When they came out they paused and sniffed for a moment or two before hopping off, just as Albert had described.

Albert had a small, round pebble ready in the sling and with a deft movement of his wrist he shot the pebble, aiming straight at the rabbit's head. It fell instantly. Still moving quietly, he collected the animal and made sure it was dead. He didn't want to cause any suffering to the rabbit.

"So you see Ben, you will be helping to win the war by killing a few rabbits. That's why I'm giving you my catapult. Think of it as your gun!"

Then Ben understood that it was important for him to help his family in this way. Rabbit was healthy meat and it might save his mum worrying so much about food. With Albert's help he practised and practised using the catapult, and eventually killed his first rabbit! He felt proud when his brother praised him.

"Well done! You're pretty good for a ten-year-old!" he said. "But now I've got to teach you the nasty bit. We have to take the skin off and gut it and it is a bit messy. I do it here in the field because then I can leave the insides for the birds and the foxes, to help feed them. Watch carefully how I skin it. If you skin it well, the skins can be dried and used to make mittens or bonnets for children. I'm sure Sid's mum would love some rabbit skins to make warm mittens for her little children in the winter."

The thought of helping Sid's family made Ben watch carefully as Albert skinned and then cleaned the rabbit. He demonstrated twice, and then helped Ben to do the one which he had killed. Ben managed quite well considering it was his first attempt. "You did well, Ben," said Albert as they took the rabbits back to the cottage. "Mum will be pleased and you can have rabbit stew tomorrow for supper!" Indeed their mother was very pleased. She smiled to see her youngest son growing up so quickly and willing to help out.

The next day everyone was up early. It was hard to say goodbye to Albert. It felt strange, too, knowing he would be just a few miles away while he was training. At least they might get to see him a few times before he was posted abroad.

After Albert left, Ben took his slate* and began to

walk to school. He had already put his lunch money and the secret message in his trouser pocket. He wanted to try and work out what the rhyme meant at playtime with Sid. The boys had a separate playground from the girls and infants, so they would have to pick Vera's brains later.

The children lined up and marched into school when the whistle blew, looking like soldiers doing drill! As always, school began with assembly where the whole school sang a hymn, and one of the teachers said prayers. Since the war had begun they prayed for the men who were away fighting for their country, and that the war would end soon. After prayers, before they were dismissed to their classes, the headmaster wished to talk to them.

"I have something to say to you all," he said, getting up on the platform. "In a few moments you will go to your classes and write on your slates a message for your parents. You will see that many children have not come to school today. It is because they are sick with an infectious illness called Belgian Flush*. It is spreading so quickly that I have decided to close the school for a week, in an attempt to stop the infection. Once you have copied the message to your parents, then you may go home and return next Monday morning."

One young lad put up his hand. "Yes Alan," the head said. "What do you want to ask?"

"Please sir, does that mean we have no penny dinners today?"

"I'm afraid it does. I am sorry about that, but we have to stop the spread of the disease."

Everyone groaned. Since the government had very recently introduced the penny dinners for school-children, many of them had more to eat than they had had for months. Now they would have a whole week of being hungry and maybe not having anything but bread and perhaps a few vegetables in a stew.

Slate pencils were given out by the class monitor and the children copied out the message to their parents. Then they were dismissed. Ben and Sid whooped in delight. A whole week of holiday!

"But think of those poor children with that awful infection," Vera said. Ben and Sid exchanged guilty glances.

"At least now we'll have time to find out the meaning of the message," said Sidney. "We'll take the little 'uns home and see if we can go to Weymouth together. Your mum will let you, won't she?"

"I expect so. She won't want me around today; it's washing day and she's always busy and a bit bad-tempered," said Ben.

"Our Mum, too," said Vera, with a sigh. "But I may have to stay at home and take care of the others."

Ben's mother was very surprised to see him arrive back home so soon.

"You've not been up to anything and got excluded have you?" she asked.

"Of course not, Mum," he answered. "It's because

there's a disease called Belgian Flush that's all round the school. Look, here's the message from the teacher, copied on my slate."

Actually, Ben's mum could barely read, but she was too ashamed to admit that to her young son, so she just glanced at the message. "Leave it there for your dad to see after work. I've never heard of such an illness in all my life. Are you sure it isn't some sort of prank you're up to?"

"No Mum. It's a real illness, honest. You get a temperature and a rash, and our teacher explained that it used to be called German measles, but now it has a new name as people don't want to use the word 'German' any more."

"Oh. Well, what are you going to do all day? I have my washing to do. You can turn the mangle handle for me if you like."

"If I do that for a bit, can I then go to Weymouth with Sid? I'll use my dinner penny to get something to eat."

"I won't have time to make you anything until supper, when we are going to have your rabbit stew. Help me with the mangle for ten minutes, and then off you go!"

Ten minutes later Ben was running down the road to Chickerell with his penny in his pocket. He burst into Mr. Savage's shop and gave a grin. "A pennyworth of peppermints please," he said.

"It's not Saturday! What's all this about?" asked the shopkeeper.

Ben told him all about the Belgian Flush and school being closed. "My friend Sid and his sister and I are going to Weymouth," he said. "The peppermints will keep us going."

"Then I'll just pop in a couple of extras for your friends," said the kind old man. And you can have one of yesterday's buns* each, too, thrown in!"

"Oh, thanks soooo much, Mr Savage!" Ben was delighted, and he knew Sid and Vera would be, too.

"I have to look after my best peppermint customer, don't I?" laughed the shopkeeper as Ben rushed out of the shop in delight and made his way to Sidney's home.

Mr. Savage was too old to go and fight in the war. As a young man he had served in the Boer War in South Africa. He had hated all the bloodshed and was glad that now he could just look after his little village shop. He lived upstairs, over the shop, all alone. His wife had died some years before.

Chapter Four

It was a long way to walk from Chickerell to Wyke, but Ben was used to it. And it gave him time to think about things. It was almost lunch time when he reached Sid and Vera's house and his stomach was making protesting noises. The twins had been helping their mother with the laundry, so she was happy to let them go to Weymouth with Ben.

In great excitement the three of them set off along the Wyke Road, munching on the buns with relish. There were a few currants in them and they tasted so good! Then they all had a peppermint.

"Mum let me keep my dinner penny," explained Ben. "So I bought a pennyworth of peppermints."

Soon they were at the end of the long Wyke Road and turning down to Rodwell. On the corner was the workhouse*. It looked so grim with its high grey walls, made of Portland stone; like a prison. Vera shivered.

"I hope we never end up living there!" she said. "Mum was there when she was a girl and she tells us terrible stories about it. She prays that Dad will never have to go to fight in the war, because she wouldn't have enough money to manage on her own. She always worries that we will get sick, too, and she wouldn't have any money to pay for a doctor to make us better. That happened to her mum, and her four brothers died in the workhouse from consumption*."

"But your dad has an important job making torpedoes, doesn't he? Why would he get sent to fight?" asked Ben.

"Well, he shouldn't have to," said Sid with a sigh. "Even so, some people think he must be a coward. A white feather was pushed through the door last week. Mum was upset about that, too. Poor mum, she worries about everything these days."

By now the children had walked down Boot Hill and were by the harbour. Ben sniffed the air appreciatively. "I love the smells of the harbour," he said. "It smells of fish and tar and salt! Let's sit on the wall and try to work out the mystery poem from the bottle. I've been thinking about it a lot. Please would you read it out, Vera?" Ben handed the paper to her.

"Whoever finds this – rich or poor,
Washed up, I hope, upon the shore,
Near a fleet where no fleet can sail,
Near a port from whence the plague did hail …"

"That first bit is easy," interrupted Sid. "We all know the Fleet, where no fleet of boats could sail."

"And of course Weymouth is the town where the plague began," added Vera.

"Is it?" asked Ben. "I knew it was something to do with rats jumping off a boat, but wasn't sure where."

"Our Vera is the clever one!" said Sid. "She remembers everything the teacher tells us. One day I reckon she'll be a teacher herself!" He gave his sister a friendly nudge, but she just sighed.

"I wish I could be, but there's not much chance of that happening. I'll have to leave school soon as I'm fourteen and get a job, like your Molly did. Anyway, here's the next bit of the poem ... There is a village which rhymes with hole," Vera read, and paused for thought. "Mm, let me see, a village name that rhymes with hole ..."

"I've been racking my brains all day about that. I can only think of Bradpole," said Ben. "You know, that village over Bridport way."

"That's a long way from Fleet and Weymouth, though," reasoned Sid. "The poem says 'near'. We need to find a map and look at the village names."

"That's a great idea!" said Ben. "But where can we find a map?"

"I know!" said Vera. "What about the railway station? They have a map on the wall of all the places where the train stops."

"Brilliant, sis!" her brother said. "Come on, let's go to the station. I just love to watch the engines, anyway – we might be lucky and see one come in or go out."

It took the children about ten minutes to reach the station and they ran into the waiting room to look at the map. Several branch lines went from Weymouth to surrounding villages, as well as the main line which went to London.

"Look, there's one!" exclaimed Sid. "Radipole!"

Ben laughed. "Of course! How stupid can I be? My sister is in service at Radipole – it's much nearer to the Fleet and Weymouth than Bradpole. That must be where we've got to beware of a mole in the churchyard!"

Just as the children were deciding whether they had time to walk out to Radipole to look for moles, a loud whistle told them that a train was coming in. They raced out of the waiting room to watch it arrive, smoke belching out from the engine like some huge monster. The noise was deafening – steam hissing and brakes squealing. The train stopped just before the buffers at the end of the platform. Weymouth was the end of the line, apart from the boat train, which took passengers to the harbour, to catch the paddle steamer to the Channel Islands.

Lots of people were getting off the train. Some people had porters to carry their luggage, but some were managing by themselves. One poor mother was struggling with two small children and a suitcase, and Vera ran to help her lift the children down from the carriage.

"Thank you, my dear," the lady said. "Do you happen to know where Avenue Road is? I need the Sunny Side Guest House."

Vera thought for a moment. "I'm not quite sure. I'll

ask my brother and his friend." She ran to the boys. Sid had no idea, but Ben knew exactly where the road was, so the three children decided to guide the lady there as it was too complicated to explain the route. Sid carried the case, Vera held the hand of one child and the mother took the other, while Ben led the way. It took them about twenty minutes to get there as the two little ones couldn't walk very quickly. They found the guest house easily as it had a bright red door and a post with a name plate swinging in the breeze. The mother was so grateful that she opened her purse and gave the children a threepenny piece each.

"We can't take your money!" exclaimed Ben, and the others shook their heads, too.

"We're just glad we could help, and we were walking back to the town anyway," said Vera, but the lady insisted. After she had gone into the house, the children stared at their coins with wide eyes. A whole threepenny piece each!

"Come on, let's go down to the beach and have an ice cream cornet," suggested Sid, breaking into a run. "I've never been as rich as this! We can also ride home on old Tom's cart for a ha'pence each, instead of walking all the way, and we'll still have lots left over! Yippee!"

"That's a great idea," agreed Ben, his eyes shining. "Beat you to the beach!"

"I feel sorry for the children in our school who have got the Belgian whatever it is," said Vera, as the three of them sat on the pebbles licking their ice-creams. "What a lovely treat this is. It's like the summer holidays!"

"Mmm," Ben agreed, absorbed in enjoying every lick of his fast-melting ice cream. "I can't remember the last time I had an ice cream. But whenever it was, this one has to be the best I've ever tasted!"

"Shall we go to Radipole tomorrow?" suggested Sid. "We haven't really got time today. We could walk across the fields and down Radipole Lane into the village and see if they have any moles in the churchyard."

"We could ask our dad about moles," said Vera. "He used to know a mole catcher who worked on a big country estate."

"Talking about catching things, Albert showed me last night how to catch rabbits and even gave me his catapult. I have to help provide meat for the family," Ben said proudly, wiping the last traces of ice-cream from his mouth with his hand. "I have to learn to skin the rabbits and gut them. It's a really horrible job, but I'm fighting the Germans now, who are trying to starve us all!"

"Mmm," said Sid, licking his lips. "Rabbit stew, delicious! It would be great if you could get a rabbit for us sometimes. We hardly ever have meat. Our mum would be ever so pleased."

"Of course I will, Sid. I'm going to save the skins for your mum to make mittens for the little ones, too."

"She'd love that," said Vera. "She's clever at sewing."

Sid nodded. "Maybe you could teach me to catch rabbits, too? Oh, but I haven't got a catapult!"

"We'll have to look for a Y shaped piece of driftwood, and try to make one," said Ben. "I'm not an expert yet, but it would be fun to teach you what Albert taught me. We could go out together!"

It was such fun riding home on Old Tom's cart. He ran a sort of bus service between Weymouth, Wyke, Charlestown and Chickerell. It wasn't very special, just a rickety wagon drawn by his old horse, but it was a great help to the villagers who needed a ride. It was a huge treat for the children. They paid their halfpenny each and it was heaps better than a hot and tiring walk uphill.

On the way home they discussed their new-found wealth. They had spent one threepenny bit on ice creams and the cart ride, so had sixpence left from the money the lady had given them. Ben had spent his dinner penny on peppermints, but Sid and Vera still had theirs, so altogether they had eight pence. It seemed like a fortune to them!

"Let's keep it for now, for expenses," suggested Sid. "After all, we are proper detectives now. If at the end we have some left over, then we could buy something for our mums."

"Good idea," said Ben. "If we really are detectives, though, we should have a name for ourselves."

"I think we should be called the Peppermint Detective Agency since Ben always shares his peppermints with us and they help us to think," suggested Vera. The boys thought it was a brilliant name.

"Then I propose that Ben is the treasurer of the Peppermint Detective Agency, because now he has a bedroom of his own and can keep the money safe," said Sid.

Vera added, "I second that." She wasn't really sure what it meant, but knew it was something which happened when committees decided things.

When they reached Wyke, Ben waved goodbye to Sid and Vera and then went the last bit of the journey on his own. In his mind he was "counting his blessings" as his dad had always taught him to do. Sometimes his dad sang the hymn, "Count your blessings, name them one by one, and it will surprise you what the Lord has done!" His dad had added a second verse, which he'd made up that went: "Count your blessings, name them two by two, and it will surprise you what the Lord can do!"

There have been many blessings recently, Ben thought, as the horse jogged him up and down in the rickety cart. Albert won't go abroad for a while; I haven't caught the Belgian Flush; we have a holiday for a week; Mr. Savage gave me some extra sweets and buns; Vera was allowed to come out as well as Sid and she's so clever at working things out; we helped the lady at the station and she gave us each a threepenny bit; we had a delicious ice cream and paddled; we could come home by Old Tom's cart *and* I belong to the Peppermint Detective Agency!

Old Tom pulled up at the top of the lane that led to Ben's home just as he was whispering "thank you" to

God. He jumped off the cart and sang the old hymn as he ran down the lane to the cottage. He felt so happy!

But his happiness evaporated when he walked in the back door. He knew something was wrong straight away. Mum was sitting at the kitchen table with her head in her hands and tears were pouring down her face. Dad was looking at her very sadly, holding a letter in his hands. Whatever had happened? Ben's stomach lurched and his heart started thumping in his chest. It must be bad news from his big brother, Fred. He must have been killed fighting the Germans.

Chapter Five

"What's going on? Has something terrible happened to Fred? He hasn't been killed has he? Or been injured?" The questions kept tumbling out of Ben's mouth as he looked from one parent to the other.

"No son. It's not as bad as that," said his dad, putting his arm around Ben. "As far as we know, Fred is just fine. I've just had a letter from the War Office, telling me that I have to go and fight. So many younger men have sadly been killed or wounded and they need us older men now to go and help with the war. These are my call up papers*."

"But why have you got to go, Dad? I thought you told me that you wouldn't have to fight because fishing was a reserved occupation* and you were providing food for people?" Ben was horrified. His dad couldn't leave them! Then he was suddenly struck with the awful realisation that with Albert going away, it would only be he and his mum left at home.

His mum continued to cry and Ben went and hugged her. "I'll look after you, Mum, I promise," he said, trying to sound brave, but his voice was quivering.

"The thing is, Ben," his dad went on to explain,

"before we moved here to be near your grandparents, I used to be a coal miner. It was before you were born. It was not a good life, working in the mines; in fact it was quite horrible going underground all day. Very dangerous, too. I wanted better for my children, so when Grandad was thinking of retiring from fishing and gave me his boats, both the lerret and the trow*, we moved here. Now, even though both coal mining and fishing are reserved occupations, miners are very urgently needed in the fighting in France because we are experts in digging very deep tunnels through rock and in using dynamite. I can't tell you much more than that – apparently it's some kind of secret operation."

"Dad has to report in Dorchester on Wednesday. We only have one more day together!" his mum said, through her tears. "First I lose Fred, then Albert, and now your dad. All my men are going!"

"I'm still here, Mum, and I'll look after you," Ben said once again, with a bit more courage this time. He was glad to see his mum smile a little.

"Yes, and you're a good boy, but we'll have to pull in our belts a lot with no wages coming in. The army send a small allowance, but it's not as good as the men's wages, and we'll still have to pay the rent."

"We won't have to go to the workhouse, will we?" asked Ben suddenly, remembering what Vera had told him earlier.

"Of course not!" said his dad. "Don't worry, son. God will take care of us. Grandad will go back to fishing full time, with my lerret crew, you will be out getting firewood and catching rabbits, and Molly will still bring home some of her wages. Mum will try and get a job, too. You'll all be fine." He turned to his wife and added, "You haven't 'lost' your big boys, either. We all intend to come marching home when this war is over and our duty is done! We're not called 'Goodenough' for nothing. We're good enough to see this battle through!"

"If only I knew that for sure," said Ben's mum, getting up to stir the rabbit stew which was simmering on the old iron stove. Ben always thought that the big, black iron stove was like some sort of wood-eating monster. It took so much driftwood to keep it going. It was the only form of heating in the kitchen, and there was always a huge kettle boiling away on it ready to make tea at any time, and often a big pot full of stew for supper.

"Only God knows our future, and we must trust him," Dad said quietly. "Now, let's have our supper and give thanks for what we do have. Our blessings are many, and we must always remember that."

The next day Ben woke wondering if he would be able to go to Radipole to look for moles, or whether he should stay and help his mum and dad. All of the happiness which he had felt yesterday had disappeared under a big, sad cloud. He got up and looked out of the window. He could see all the way to the Fleet. The sky was grey and the sea choppy. He felt as if the sunshine had disappeared completely out of his life.

Slowly Ben dressed and went downstairs. He walked through the kitchen to the scullery and washed in the big white sink as he always did before breakfast. Then he went back to the kitchen for his big hunk of bread and glass of milk and water which his mum had put out for him.

"Can you do something for me today?" his mum asked him as he finished eating. "I know it's a bit of a walk, but maybe Sidney would go with you. Dad has written a note to our Molly to tell her that he has been called up to fight and is leaving home tomorrow. Can you take it over to Radipole for me? You must go to the back door of the house and ask politely if you can see your sister and tell them that you have an important message."

The servants had to use the back door to Radipole Manor; only the family and important guests were allowed through the front door. It wouldn't do for Ben to ring the front door bell!

"Yes mum," Ben answered. He hadn't told his mum about the bottle, but now seemed as good a time as any. "Actually," he admitted, "Sid, Vera and I were hoping to go to Radipole today, anyway, and explore. We found a bottle on Chesil beach with a message in it and are trying to work it out."

Ben's mum was only half-listening. She had a lot on her mind and thought Ben was just talking about a make-believe game, not a real message in a bottle. "Dad is coming home from work at noon and said he hoped you would be in early for your supper so that you could have a walk together before he goes away."

"Of course, Mum. I'll go to Wyke now and see if Sid and Vera can come with me and I'll be home by four, I promise."

Sid and Vera were upset for Ben when they heard about his dad. Their mother, too, was very sad to hear the news. Everything about the war made her sad. Children shouldn't have to grow up so quickly and take such responsibility.

"Be careful crossing the backwater," she called out as they set off. "Don't fall into Radipole Lake and make yourselves mucky. I know what you boys are like; you'll be trying to catch sticklebacks and things like that!"

"We won't," they called back. The backwater was a very marshy area, where once the River Wey flowed and the channel had been deep enough for ships to navigate. The children made their way carefully across the logs that made rather shaky bridges over the wet grassland.

"We'd better deliver the letter first," said Ben, stretching his arms out sideways to help steady himself on his log. "Then we can go to the churchyard and see if there are any moles." Ben quoted the poem as he now knew it by heart:

"Whoever finds this – rich or poor,
Washed up, I hope, upon the shore,
Near a fleet where no fleet can sail,
Near a port from whence the plague did hail,

There is a village which rhymes with 'hole'
And in the churchyard, beware – a mole!
Catch him and help to win the war
Find the tunnel with hidden store.
But he is cunning, so beware!
For your life, please take care."

"I asked dad about moles last night," Vera told Ben, "but he said they were very shy creatures and almost impossible to catch. It didn't seem that they were cunning or dangerous in any way. I don't know why we should have to 'beware the mole'."

Ben shook his head. "I wonder if there are any other kinds of mole apart from the brown lumps on the skin. I can't think of anything, can you?"

"Nope!" said Sid and Vera together.

It was a lovely sunny day, and the three friends sang as they walked to Radipole village, just like they had seen real soldiers do. They went straight to the big manor house where Molly worked. It was close to the church, and on the opposite side of the road was the village school. They could hear children in the playground, and realised it must be dinner time. It felt strange that other children were in school but they weren't!

"After we have delivered the message, shall we buy some bread for lunch with one of our pennies?" suggested Sid. "There must be a baker in the village."

"Yes, there is," said Ben. "I know Molly sometimes

has to go there. She has told us about it because she feels sorry for the baker's wife. The baker was German but grew up in England, as his father and mother came here many years ago. He married a local girl and they have three small children. When the war began, Mr. Smidtz changed his name to Mr. Smith. He even changed the name outside the shop. In 1914 he disappeared and people think he may have been kidnapped and taken to Germany. Mrs. Smith hasn't heard from him since. She fears he might be dead and struggles to keep the children fed and clothed as well as running the business on her own. Molly says Mrs. Smith bakes the nicest bread and tries to keep cheerful. Some people won't go to her shop, even though she is a local girl, just because she married a man who had German parents."

"Should we buy from her?" asked Vera. "We are supposed to hate all things German."

Ben looked troubled. "I don't know," he said slowly. "My dad has always told me that God loves everybody and we should love people whatever their background. It's very confusing. It's a bit like the minister's sermon last Sunday, about hating the evil rather than people. Molly certainly feels sorry for this family."

By now the children had arrived at the back door of Radipole Manor, which stood next to St. Ann's church. Ben knocked on the back door of the imposing house, holding the letter from his father in his other hand. The door opened.

"Yes my dears, what can I do for you?" asked a plump

middle-aged woman. She was dressed smartly in a striped dress, covered with an apron, and she wore a white mop cap on her head.

"Please, Ma'am," Ben said politely. "I am Molly Goodenough's brother and I have an important message for her from our dad." He handed the letter to the woman.

"Moll!" she called. "Here's a boy who says he's your brother, with a letter for you. You'd best come and see to it yourself."

Ben almost gasped out loud when he saw his sister He had never seen her in her maid's uniform. She, too, had a blue striped dress covered by a very large apron, and wore a white headdress which kept her hair tidy. She looked very smart!

Molly frowned when she saw Ben there. "What are you doing here, Ben?" she asked. "It's not bad news of our Fred is it?"

"No Molly," Ben said at once, "but it's not very good news, either. Dad's got to go to France to fight."

"He's got to what?" asked Molly, taking the letter from Ben. Her hand was shaking, and it gave Ben a lump in his throat. He swallowed hard.

"Why don't you bring the children in while you read the letter?" suggested the plump woman who they later learnt was the cook. She looked at the children kindly. "You all look tired and thirsty. Have you walked all the way over here?"

"Yes Ma'am," Vera answered politely.

The kitchen was the biggest kitchen Ben had ever

seen. On one side there was an enormous cooking range, which was black and shiny. On it were several saucepans as well as a large kettle. It must take forests of wood to keep that alight, thought Ben to himself.

One wall was full of shelves which contained bowls and dishes of all shapes and sizes, and there was also a rack full of bottles of herbs and spices. Many spoons and other kitchen utensils hung from hooks on the wall. Onions were hanging from one hook in the ceiling, and bacon from another. There was a wonderful smell of cooking and despite everything, Ben couldn't help sniffing appreciatively!

Near the door which led out of the kitchen, a long line of bells hung on the wall. They were all labelled. To take his mind off the letter, Ben read the names above each one, like "dining room", "front parlour" and "bedroom one". It was all very interesting – like another world. He had never seen a kitchen like it!

In the centre of the kitchen was a long, scrubbed wooden table, with chairs all round it. Molly sat at the table and read the letter slowly, trying not to cry, while the cook brought out soup and rolls for the children. It was awesome to be given a free lunch in that amazing kitchen!

"I think I'll ask Her Ladyship if I can have the rest of the day off," Molly said to the cook, looking up from the letter. Her voice wobbled a bit. "My dad is being sent to the war, tomorrow! He's been urgently called up to help with some special operation in France. He used to be a miner. It's all to do with his skills with detonating explosives. He wants to say goodbye, because he may not see me for a long time …" Tears came to her eyes and Cook patted Molly's shoulder.

"You stay there my dear, I'll go and tell her Ladyship what's happened."

The children all stood up quickly when Lady Worthington entered the kitchen a minute later. Ben wasn't quite sure if he should bow or not, because she looked so elegant, like royalty. Her clothes were rich and fine, and she was even wearing a gold necklace in the morning!

The lady smiled kindly at the children and told them to sit down and finish their soup while she took Molly upstairs to talk about the situation.

Molly came back just as Ben, Vera and Sid were finishing their soup. "Her Ladyship says I can go home this afternoon and come back tomorrow afternoon. I can leave at three. What are you all going to do? Do you want to wait for me? We're allowed to go back in the pony and trap."

"Wow! We get to ride in a real pony and trap?" Sid asked in great excitement. "We'll stay!"

"Actually, Molly," said Ben, "we want to have a look around the churchyard while we are over here. We want to look for moles."

"Moles?" asked Cook in astonishment. "Whatever for? I don't think you'll find any moles out there. But there is a ghost, an old man in a long, black hooded robe. He usually only gets seen in the evening. Once the choirboys saw him when they came for practice. They were scared stiff and all ran away!"

"A ghost?" Vera exclaimed. "I don't think I want to see a ghost!" She gave a little shiver of fear. Was there really a ghost in the churchyard? Ben wondered. He had only heard of such things in stories.

The children thanked Cook very much for the delicious soup and rolls and promised to be back in good time. They had no watches, but the church clock struck every quarter of an hour, so they would listen for the quarter to three chime.

There were two churchyards at the quaint old church of St. Ann's. The children headed for the older one around the church first. "Do you think the cook was teasing us about a ghost?" asked Vera, as they began their search for molehills.

"I don't think there's such a thing as ghosts – mind you, I can't see any molehills here either," said Sid, as the three of them ran round the churchyard.

After they had criss-crossed the whole churchyard and not found even a hint of a molehill, Ben suggested, "Shall we try the other one?" The second churchyard was over the road, right next to the school playground, but that search revealed nothing either, which was really disappointing. They searched both churchyards a second time, even in the brambles and bushes, and behind every tree. Just as they were about to give up, Ben halted in his tracks.

"Shh," he said suddenly. "I think I heard something rustling in the bushes over there. Look!"

Sid and Vera turned towards where he was pointing. From within the bushes they caught a glimpse of something black. What could it be?

Chapter Six

Vera looked as if she was about to scream, so Sid covered her mouth. Ben ducked behind the nearest gravestone. Sid and Vera joined him, and they all peered out. A second later, a black cat jumped out and ran away – with a mouse in its mouth! The three of them grinned at each other, feeling a bit embarrassed.

"A cat, but still no moles," sighed Ben in disappointment. "I really thought we would find some molehills. At least there wasn't a ghost!"

"Perhaps we should just give up on the clues and hand the paper to someone like the village policeman. He would be able to contact Captain Wray's wife," suggested Sid, sitting on a bench. "That's if she really exists," he added with a sigh.

Vera nodded. "Maybe the poem doesn't really mean anything after all. Maybe it wasn't really written by a man called Captain Wray."

Sid looked sideways at Vera and gave her a friendly punch. "Maybe you're still recovering from the shock we've just had, thinking the cat was a ghost," he teased.

She pulled a face. "You were just as scared too," she said.

"Was not!"

"Were!"

"Was not!"

"Oh, do stop, you two," Ben said. "Here, let's have a peppermint each, that will help us think." He handed the bag round, and they sat in silence for a minute. "I know – as we've got some time left, let's go into the village and see if we can buy some of yesterday's buns. We don't need lunch for ourselves, but we could take them back as a treat for your brothers and sisters?"

"That would be lovely," said Vera, standing up and stretching. "We can think while we walk." They set off down the hill and over the bridge into the centre of the village, where they quickly found the baker's shop. The bell rang when they opened the door and a young woman came from a room at the back to serve them. They guessed it must be Mrs. Smith. She smiled and asked the children what they wanted.

"Do you have a pennyworth of buns or cakes left from yesterday, please?" asked Vera.

"Well dear, I have some of my famous Portland dough cake. It's made from a recipe my granny gave me. Would that do?" asked Mrs. Smith with a smile.

"Oh yes, please! Portland dough cake is our mum's favourite!" said Vera.

Mrs. Smith filled a bag with pieces of dough cake and the children thanked her. Ben produced the penny to pay for it. They couldn't resist sharing a piece between them. Even though it had been made the day before, it still tasted delicious!

The children walked slowly back to the manor house. As they approached the church, Ben suddenly had a desire to go in on his own. He couldn't really explain why and he felt a bit shy about telling his friends. But the feeling persisted.

"I'm just going to pop in here for a minute," he mumbled and ran inside the church before they could ask any awkward questions.

The church was cool inside and the sunlight was dancing through the windows. Ben felt contented and he suddenly knew why he was there. He sat down in a pew at the back, and then knelt down to pray, like they did in the church services on Sundays. "Dear God," he said. "I know you know everything. So I was just wondering whether you could help us to work out what this poem means. Oh, and please keep everyone safe, because the poem says 'beware'. Amen."

As Ben left the church, the clock struck quarter to three. He quickly joined the others and they walked next door to Radipole Manor. Molly was waiting for them, and after a couple of minutes the pony and trap drew up outside.

"This is David," Molly said, introducing the children to the young lad who was driving. "And this is Ben, my brother, and his friends, Sid and Vera." David grinned at the children in a friendly way and lifted his smart hat to them. Ben decided he liked him straight away.

David looked very impressive dressed in his livery*. His black trousers with a red stripe down the outside of each leg and red jacket with gold braid and shiny bright buttons reminded Ben of toy soldiers!

Molly climbed up beside David and the children climbed on to the wooden seat behind them. Ben felt like a king sitting so high up, watching the familiar landmarks go by. David drove them the long way round, just for fun. They went all round the harbour, up Boot Hill and along the Wyke Road. Then he pointed out where his mum lived. Ben was surprised when he saw tears in David's eyes. "My dad died about two years ago. My mum was devastated. We both were. Now I work at the Manor and give most of my wages to my mum. You have to appreciate your family as much as you can while you still have them, because you never know how long you will have them for."

Ben's eyes also filled with tears as he remembered he would be saying goodbye to his dad when he got home.

Their father was busy packing a small suitcase when Ben and Molly ran in. "Oh, Molly, I'm so happy you could get some time off to say goodbye!" he said, giving Molly a big hug.

Although Dad tried to be cheerful at tea time, they all knew, deep down inside, that there was a very real chance that he would not survive the war. Every day there were so many casualties; every week at church there was a new list of names of dead and injured men.

After tea, Ben's dad wanted to take a last look at the stretch of water he loved so much and invited Ben to go with him. Ben's dad untied the trow and rowed them over to Chesil Beach. They climbed over the ridge of pebbles to the shore, and then played a game together, skimming flat pebbles across the water, seeing which would go the furthest. It was a game they had played as long as Ben could remember.

"I wanted a little time with my youngest son alone," his dad said. "I had hoped that you would have been able to enjoy a little more childhood than I did, Ben. I was sent down the mines when I was your age. It was horrible and it wasn't fair, but that was the way it was back then. Everyone was so poor. Now, at least you can stay at school until you are fourteen. I hope you might do well and get a scholarship to the grammar school, if this war ends soon. In the meantime you will be the man of the house, and I need you to look after mum for us all."

"I will, Dad, you know I will. I will catch rabbits, collect firewood and do anything else I can," said Ben.

"I know you will, son. I'm proud of you; you are a good boy. However, I don't want to go away without giving you something." His dad put his hand into the breast pocket of his jacket and pulled out a New Testament.

"I was given this by a man in Somerset who used to have tent meetings for us when we were young people. He told us a lot about God's love and we learnt to trust Jesus and always follow and love Him. I want you to read a few verses every day and then pray and ask God to help you. Before you go to bed at night, pray for us all, and pray that God will forgive you for the things you've done wrong. Mum and I have always prayed together before we go to bed. Maybe you can do that instead of me?"

Ben looked at his dad as he took the little book and slipped it into his trouser pocket. His dad looked so serious he knew that what he was being told was important. He promised to try to read from the New Testament and pray each day. It was the first book he had ever owned. He held it tight. "Won't you miss having it, Dad?" he asked.

"One part of our soldier's kit is a little New Testament. We keep in the left breast pocket of our jackets. It protects our hearts in every way," answered his dad. "We are given it at the same time we get our uniform and the rest of our kit."

Ben was very quiet and thoughtful. There were questions in his mind that had troubled him for ages. Maybe he would find the answers when he read the New Testament.

"What's on your mind, son? You're looking thoughtful! Let's walk along the shore and we can have a chat. Maybe I can help?"

"Well," started Ben slowly, "I know it sounds a bit stupid, but at church, especially at Easter, we sing that hymn, 'There is a green hill far away', and there is one line I don't understand. It says 'there was no other good enough to pay the price of sin', but in our house there are six Goodenoughs, then there's grandad and grandma and there must be others with our name."

Ben's dad grinned. "Ah, I can explain that," he said. "Jesus never did anything wrong all the time he lived on this earth. He was perfect, holy and pure. He was like this because he was God's son, not just an ordinary human being like us. We all do wrong things, but he never did. He took the punishment we all deserve: the death penalty. Jesus died for us, so that his Father God could forgive us, and make us part of His family. But it doesn't just happen; we need to realise we have done wrong and ask God to forgive us, and ask Jesus to be our friend and Saviour. Jesus was the only one good enough to take the death penalty for us; that is what that hymn means."

"Thanks, Dad, I think I understand now. My other question isn't about Jesus, it's …" and Ben hesitated a little, "it's about me."

"Go on then, spill the beans," said his dad. "What about you?"

"Once, when I was about seven and in the butcher's shop a lady said I was an 'accident'. Was I really an accident, Dad? Did you and mum not really want me?"

Ben's dad put his arm around him. "Ben, you may have been a bit of a surprise to your mum and me when we found out that you were on the way. A surprise, but an especially wonderful surprise! We were so delighted and excited! No child is an 'accident' to God. Each one is special and God has planned its birth and life. You were such a special gift that we called you Benjamin, which means, 'the child of our old age'. Indeed, Ben, what would your mum and I do now if we didn't have you, our special son? I can go away to war knowing that you are at home and mum won't be lonely and she will have some help. You are very special to us and to God, and have brought us a lot of joy, too!"

Ben looked up at his dad and smiled. "Thanks, Dad."

"Any other burning questions my special son has for me?" asked his dad.

"Well ..." Ben hesitated. "Dad, I know there are animals called moles and there are brown spots on our skin that we call moles, but are there any other sorts of moles?"

"Whatever will you ask me next?" his dad replied with a laugh. "I can only think of one other kind of mole. It is a nickname that is sometimes used for a spy. Maybe they are called that because they do hidden, underground work, like real moles."

Ben's mouth dropped open, and he felt as if his heart missed a beat. A mole was another word for a spy! He couldn't wait to tell the others! Perhaps the message was about a spy. Wow! Now they really deserved to be called the Peppermint Detective Agency.

"Anything else?" his dad asked him.

"Can I try to catch a rabbit before we go home?"

"As long as you catch one quickly, otherwise your mum will send out a search party for us!" They got up and walked back over the beach to the trow. Then Ben's dad rowed them over the Fleet back to the fields, where

Ben managed to catch a rabbit. His dad helped him skin and clean it, and they took it home as a trophy to the cottage.

"Look Mum," said Ben as he ran into the house. "See, I can look after you while Dad and Fred and Albert are away, and I will!"

Chapter Seven

The next day was one of those sad days that stay in your memory forever. Molly and Ben walked with their mother and father all the way to Weymouth train station to wave him off. They wished that Albert could been there as well but he had only been with the tank regiment for two days, so it wasn't possible. Dad was initially going to Dorchester, only six miles away, for his training, but after that he might go straight to France to do a particularly dangerous job. They weren't sure if he would be able to visit them before he went to France. In fact, they couldn't be sure they would ever see him again.

As the train pulled into the station, Ben felt as if he had a huge stone in his throat. So much was happening in their family, and so quickly that he couldn't really believe it was all true. He wished it was a dream and he would wake up and find both his brothers and his father were still at home. Ben looked at Molly, and squeezed her hand, seeing she was nearly in tears. Their mum was holding on to their dad's hand and they knew she didn't want to let it go. On the platform their dad kissed Molly, then gave Ben a bear hug, before saying his very special goodbye to their mum. All of them tried not to cry and to be brave, giving dad a smile to remember as he went away.

Once he had boarded the train, and the guard had blown his whistle, they waved and waved until the train was out of sight. As they walked off the platform all of them were very quiet. They just didn't know what to say to comfort each other. Even though the sun was shining, Ben felt cold and miserable. He talked to himself in his head, telling himself to put a brave face on and cheer his mother up. He remembered his grandad's favourite saying, "Worse things happen at sea", but he couldn't think of anything much worse at that moment.

Molly had to get back to work, but had a good idea."Let's have some chips and eat them on the beach to cheer ourselves up," she suggested. "The treat's on me. Here Ben, go to the chippy and buy us a farthing bag each, with salt and vinegar, there's a love." She handed Ben the money and took her mum to sit on the promenade.

The chips were a real treat, something they only had on rare occasions when they spent a half day holiday on the sandy beach at Weymouth. Sitting in deckchairs on the prom and looking at the glistening sea, while they munched on the chips helped Ben to feel a bit better.

"What a good job your school is closed this week," Molly said to Ben. "At least we could see Dad off." She sighed. "Now I'd better get back to the Big House. They've been so good to me, letting me have time off and lending us the pony and trap that I must make sure I'm not late." She kissed her mum and Ben, wiped her eyes, and set off.

Ben's mum sighed deeply and seemed to make a big effort to motivate herself. "Best be getting home, too, I suppose," she said.

As they drew near Wyke village, Ben had an idea. He could tell Sid and Vera that a mole was another word for a spy! "Can I go and see Sid, Mum?" Ben asked. "We're passing his house. Maybe we can go winkling* on the rocks at Ferry Bridge."

"Yes, of course, dear, but be back by six for supper."

Ben raced off. As he ran, he felt as if he was shaking off some of the sadness of the morning and the tight ball in his stomach seemed to unravel a bit. After all, saying goodbye to Dad didn't take away from the fact that he had found out what the "mole" in the poem meant! In fact, it made it special that it was his dad who had helped him. He was so excited about telling the other members of the Peppermint Detective Agency about his discovery!

Sid and Vera were out in the garden, helping their mother tend the growing vegetables. Everyone needed to grow as much food as possible, especially people with big families. Even the school playing field had been dug up! Instead of sports they now had gardening in the curriculum, much to the children's disgust! However, the drill type exercises they now did in P.E. lessons were quite fun and kept them fit and strong.

"Hello Ben. Did your dad get off all right?" Sid and Vera's mother asked.

"Yes, thanks," he answered. "We all got a bit upset, but Molly treated us to some chips! Mum said I can go winkling. Can Sid and Vera come, too?" he asked.

"As long as you get lots and we can have them for supper!" Sid's mum replied, laughing. "A bit of seafood would go down a treat!"

"I thought we could go to Ferry Bridge – it's not too far to walk and the tide will be out. Can you bring a bucket and a knife, Sid?"

As soon as the friends were on their way, Ben told them of his exciting discovery. "Last night I was talking to my dad and I asked him if he knew of any other kinds of moles besides the spots and the animals. And guess what? He told me that a mole is a nickname for a spy!"

"Wow!" said Sid, his eyes shining. "So we're looking for a spy!"

Vera gasped. "Now that bit makes sense!" she said. "The bit about catching the mole and helping the war."

The twins and Ben began to recite the poem again, together:

"Whoever finds this – rich or poor
Washed up, I hope, upon the shore,
Near a fleet where no fleet can sail,
Near a port from whence the plague did hail
There is a village which rhymes with 'hole'
And in the churchyard, beware – a mole!

Catch him and help to win the war
Find his tunnel with hidden store
But he is cunning – so beware!
For your life – please take care."

"What about the warning, though, that it could be dangerous?" said Vera. "Do you think we should tell a grown up? I mean, looking for a spy …"

Ben shrugged. "I did tell mum about the bottle, but she didn't take much notice."

"Then I think we should have a go at trying to find the tunnel and the store ourselves, and if we can't find it or have any trouble then we should get help," said Sid. The others nodded.

"Good plan," agreed Ben.

Soon they were on the shore and scrambling around the rock pools, looking for winkles and limpets. The winkles were fairly easy to pry off the rocks, but the limpets were another matter! Still, they kept at it. Sid's knife worked well, and they took it in turns to use it: it was just thin enough to get between the fish and the rock. Sid had brought quite a large tin bucket and soon it was pretty full. It was really heavy, because they had filled it with sea water, to keep the fish fresh.

When they decided they had enough, they clambered out of the rock pools and on to the dunes for a rest. "Peppermint anyone?" offered Ben, peering into his nearly empty paper bag. "There are just three left!"

"Not many ships around the harbour these days," said

Sid, looking out to Portland harbour. "It's been pretty quiet since the fleet left to go to war. There is one navy boat out there. Maybe she's refuelling or come in for repairs."

"Look over there!" said Vera, pointing further up the dunes. "There's a man taking photos of the boat. We don't see many holidaymakers these days."

As she spoke, the man got on his bike and began to ride along the narrow road to Portland. He didn't appear to have seen them. The branch line train from Portland to Weymouth whistled as it approached the bend, and the children saw the man dismount and take a photo of the train. When the train passed them, they waved to the driver and guard, who waved cheerfully back to them. It was a goods train, and the trucks were loaded with stone from the Portland quarries.

"Fancy taking a photo of a goods train," commented Sid. "What a strange thing to do."

"Maybe he collects train numbers and loves engines as much as you do!" laughed Vera.

Further up the dunes where the man had been when they first saw him, Vera could see a clump of thrift. Her mum loved the pretty pink wild flower, which locals called "sea pinks" and decided to go and pick her a bunch. "I'll pick some for your mum, too," she said to Ben. "They might cheer her up now your dad and brothers have all gone."

Vera ran off and the boys played together, popping the bladder seaweed and paddling in the shallow water.

Then they heard Vera call, "Hey boys, come and see this!"

They ran to where she was standing and saw she had a pair of gloves in her hand. "I think that man on the bike might have dropped them," she said.

"Why would anyone be wearing black winter gloves in May?" said Ben. He looked at them closely and found a label inside.

"These aren't English," he said. "The writing inside is foreign. Maybe the man is a foreigner. He's a long way away by now; he's probably in Portland already. What shall we do with them? They're awfully nice gloves!"

"If we leave them here he might come back for them," Sid suggested.

"If we leave them here someone from Whitehead's Works will pinch them for sure! They'll be coming home off their shift very soon," remarked Vera.

"Maybe we should take them to the policeman in Chickerell," said Ben. "He might not be very interested with war work keeping him busy, but we can try. Usually he just keeps lost items at the police house for three months and then, if nobody collects them, he gives them back to the person who found them."

So the children took the gloves back with them, taking turns to carry the heavy bucket of shellfish. At Sid and Vera's house they put some of the shellfish into a smaller bucket for Ben to give to his mum to cook. He also took the gloves and the bunch of flowers Vera had picked. Normally he would have felt a bit of a sissy carrying flowers, but he didn't mind for once as he wanted to cheer his mum up.

On the way home a sudden thought came to him. Could the man on the bike have been a spy? Somewhere in the back of his mind he remembered hearing that German spies were taking photos of naval defences around the coast. But then, he reasoned, goods trains were hardly coastal defences, were they? It was all a bit of a mystery.

After he had gone to bed that evening Ben remembered what his dad had asked him to do. Even this very first day he had failed. He hadn't read anything from the New Testament or talked to God. He felt miserable, not at all "special" like Dad had said he was.

Well, there was still something he could do. He got out of bed and crept downstairs. His mum was darning a sock in the light of the oil lamp. "What's up, Ben?" she asked. "Are you finding it hard to go to sleep?"

"No Mum. It's just that Dad said we should say prayers together like he used to with you. I forgot."

Tears welled up in his mum's eyes. "Yes love, we could do that."

Ben went over to sit next to her and she took his hands in hers and said a prayer thanking God for all his help through the day, even though it had been so hard to say goodbye to Dad, and for giving them food and good health. Then she prayed for safety for Fred living in the trenches, for Albert in his training camp and for Ben's dad as he began his square bashing* for the war.

Then she thanked God for Ben and asked for him to be blessed.

Ben wasn't very sure what it meant to be "blessed", but it seemed to be something people said in their prayers all the time. He said "amen" at the end and then they prayed the Lord's Prayer together, which Ben knew by heart. His mum hugged him and he went up to bed feeling better. Soon he fell fast asleep dreaming of soldiers eating winkles and chips!

Chapter Eight

The day after his dad's enlistment, Ben's life changed for ever. It was as if he had to grow up overnight. It began with Mum's big announcement at breakfast.

"Ben," she said, nervously fiddling with the cutlery, "I have had to make a very difficult decision. With Albert and Dad now in the army as well as Fred, I shall have to earn some money. The payment I will receive from the army will not be anything like as much as their wages. Also, I will have far less work to do at home, so feel I should do my bit for the war effort, too. I am going to ask for a job* in the factory the other side of Chickerell where they are making ammunition."

Ben stared at her in horror. "But mums don't work*!"

"They didn't used to, but they do now there's a war on," his mum said firmly.

"But you do your bit already by knitting socks and balaclava hats for the men in the trenches. Isn't that enough? Dad didn't want you to go to work in munitions!"

"I know. But things are different now. Things have changed for all of us. I have made my mind up and am going to see the manager this morning. It is the best paid job that a woman can get these days and I'll be helping to win this terrible war! I'll tell you how I get on at dinner time. Meanwhile, the broad beans are growing nicely, but they need weeding. Would you mind doing that for me?"

"Of course I will, Mum," Ben answered, "but may I go to Chickerell first? Sid, Vera and I found a pair of gloves when we were at Ferry Bridge, and we thought we ought to hand them in at the police house as lost property because they are very smart ones."

"Certainly, I'm glad you're honest enough to do that. As you're going to the village please could you also buy two rashers of bacon from Mr. Savage's shop for our supper?"

Ben was bewildered and upset about his mum getting a job. He had heard so many bad reports about working conditions in the munitions factory and workers becoming ill. Also, mum had always been at home for him. What would he do if she had to work late or on night shifts? He didn't fancy being in the cottage on his own; it was right down a lane with no other houses nearby. These thoughts kept whirling around his head as he walked into Chickerell.

His first call was at the police house. It had a large porch which doubled up as an office when need be. Ben told the constable about the suspicious-looking man taking photos, finding the gloves in the spot where he'd been, and the label in the gloves being in a foreign language.

The constable wrote everything down. "Very sensible you are, young Ben. I'll lock them up in my cupboard for now and inform the sergeant in Weymouth. He can decide if anything else needs to be done. There may be spies anywhere, and we must be careful. Maybe he wanted to spy on Whitehead's torpedo works. Anyway, thank you and if anything comes of it all, I'll tell you."

Ben wondered if he should tell the constable about the message in the bottle, but hesitated. He hadn't consulted the others in the Peppermint Detective Agency, and anyway, if he came up with yet another spy story, maybe the policeman would think he was just making things up!

Next, Ben went to Mr. Savage's shop. It was the sort of shop that sold everything from bread and milk to matches and paraffin. Even though there was a butcher's shop in Chickerell, Mr. Savage sold bacon and meat pies. The shop had a wonderful smell – a mixture of all these things. Ben always loved going to the shop – it felt a comfortable place to be.

"You can't want more peppermints already!" the shopkeeper exclaimed, looking up when Ben came through the door.

"No," replied Ben. "Mum wants two rashers of bacon for our supper, please."

"Only two?" said a surprised Mr. Savage. "Normally she gets one for each of you."

"This week Albert has gone to Bovington to train to be a tank soldier. Dad got his papers, too, and he left yesterday. So there's only two of us now, and even Mum is going to see about a job in the munitions factory, to do her bit for the war effort."

"My goodness!" exclaimed Mr. Savage. "Where will it all end? Now that makes you the man of the house. Next thing will be that you will be asking me if I have any work for you!"

"I wish you did," said Ben, "then maybe Mum could stay at home!"

Mr. Savage looked thoughtful. "Can you ride a bike, Ben? If you can, you could help me with deliveries on Saturday mornings, if you like. I could do with a hand."

Ben's face fell. "I've never ridden a bike and we haven't got one anyway, so I can't learn. In fact, I don't know anyone who does have a bike." His face suddenly brightened. "I could carry some of your deliveries around the village, though, if you like?"

"We'll have a think about it, Ben. I tell you what, though, I could do with a bit of help this afternoon, if you are free and your mum agrees. It's half day closing and I have to go to Sturminster mill to buy flour. The milkman lets me use his horse and cart once he has finished his deliveries. The flour is heavy but with you and me lifting the sacks together it would be much easier! How about it? I shall leave promptly at half past two but we won't be back until half past six or seven o'clock."

Ben's eyes widened. "I'd love to come and help, Mr. Savage! Going to Sturminster Newton would be such an adventure – I've never been that far in my life! I'll ask my mum when she comes back from her interview. I do hope she lets me!"

Ben kept his promise to his mum and weeded the vegetable garden when he got back. He felt much more himself again with the possibility of riding over to Sturminster mill that afternoon with Mr. Savage. He began to sing "Count your blessings" as he worked. Suddenly he made the connection between "blessings" – all the good things which happened – and what it meant for God to bless him. God wanted to fill his life with good things, even when there were bad things happening.

Weeding gave Ben time to think. He thought about pulling up the weeds so that the vegetables could grow properly. He realised that in his own life there were quite a lot of things that were like weeds. They choked out the blessings God wanted to give him. He knew he was sometimes mean and unkind and selfish. He didn't always tell the truth, either, and once he had pinched a few sweets from Mr. Savage's shop counter. Remembering that made him feel very ashamed, because Mr. Savage had always been so kind to him.

His mum came home bubbling over with excitement! She was thrilled when Ben made her a cup of tea, and sat down to tell him about her interview.

"I can start work on Monday when you go back to school," she said, sipping her tea. "The manager was very understanding and has promised that I can just do daytime shifts so I don't have to leave you alone at night. I was worried about that."

"So was I," admitted Ben. "It would be lonely in the cottage on my own, especially in winter."

"I will earn a good wage, even though it is half what the men earn. They will give me a uniform to wear so my clothes won't be spoilt. He even said that I can have Saturday afternoon off as well as Sunday. I can tell you, Ben, I'm really excited!"

"I'm glad Mum. I have some news, too. I went to the police house and the constable has taken the gloves into safe keeping. He said I was right to take them in. Then, when I got the bacon from Mr. Savage, he wondered if I could go with him to Sturminster Newton mill this afternoon, by horse and cart, to help him with the heavy sacks of flour. Can I go, Mum? Please!"

"Goodness, that's a long way, all the way to Sturminster Newton! I don't see why not, though. Did he say what time you would be back?"

"Probably not until seven. Is that all right? We have to leave at 2.30pm sharp."

"I'll tell you what, then, I'll cook that bacon now and we can have bacon and eggs for dinner. Then you can just have some bread for supper when you get in."

It was a lovely dinner and Ben was very excited about his trip. This was going to be a real adventure! He ran so fast back to Chickerell that he was there ten minutes early.

"Ready for your trip, then?" asked Mr. Savage,

smiling. "You can start by giving Brownie his bag of oats. He's already harnessed up to the cart. Just put this feed bag over his head. He's a very gentle horse, but quite old now. He'll need a good feed before we set off."

"Mum got the job! She's ever so excited! She starts on Monday when I go back to school," Ben said as Mr. Savage handed him the horse's nose bag.

Mr. Savage smiled at Ben, a bit sadly. "I'm glad it went well," he replied, then sighed. "Let's hope this war is over soon, though, so we don't need ammunition any more."

Ben nodded. "Yes, that would be good. Then my dad and Fred and Albert can come home, too." He took the bag of oats outside to Brownie, who was standing quietly in the shafts of the cart waiting to go. Ben was used to Brownie. She came down the lane to his house every morning with the milkman, bringing the milk. It was Ben's job to run out with the milk jug. The milkman would measure out the number of pints with a metal cup on a long handle. Ben almost always talked to Brownie, and in the autumn would give him fallen apples from the tree in the back garden.

Brownie neighed as Ben gave him his oats, and Ben stroked his nose. He wished he had an apple to give him now. "Brownie, I'm coming with you to the mill to get the flour!" he whispered to the horse. "Won't that be fun!"

Chapter Nine

Ben felt very important sitting beside Mr. Savage as they rode in the horse and cart. They trotted along the lanes out of Weymouth, through Dorchester and then on to the Yeovil road. Soon they turned off to go towards the town of Sherborne. Almost every village had a water trough somewhere by the roadside, so horses could stop and have a drink. Very few cars ever travelled through the villages, but there were lots of horses and carts.

Whenever they stopped for Brownie to drink, it was Ben's job was to shovel up the manure that the horses left behind. There was a bucket and a shovel kept in the back of the cart for this. Once rotted down, manure was dug into the vegetable patches and helped to replenish the nutrients in the soil, so it was very useful!

"You can have some of it to enrich your mum's garden," Mr. Savage said, and Ben knew she would be very pleased, even though it did smell really bad!

As they went along, Mr. Savage pointed out things of interest to his young companion. "See that tiny little pub over there? It's the smallest in England … now this village we're passing through is called Cerne Abbas; there was a monastery here once … and see there on the hillside?" Mr. Savage pointed out a huge man drawn in the chalk. "It was done so long ago no one is sure exactly when."

In almost every village and town they saw a soldier or two in uniform, no doubt home for a few days' leave. Apart from that it was so peaceful no one would ever have dreamt there was a war going on.

At one farm, they stopped for Mr. Savage to buy eggs to sell in his shop. The farmer's wife gave Ben a drink of milk straight from the cow. He was used to milk from his local farm, but this was warm, creamy and even more delicious! Somehow, on that lovely afternoon, everywhere looked especially beautiful and smelt wonderful. The farmyard smelt of animals, but it was a clean sort of smell. Ben sighed in contentment, as he wiped the milk from his mouth.

It took two hours to arrive at their destination, but for Ben the time seemed to pass quickly, with all the things to look at from high up on his seat on the cart. When they were going along a straight bit of road with nothing coming the other way, Mr. Savage had even allowed him to take the reins and taught him how to drive the cart. Ben felt very proud to be trusted to do that!

When they reached the mill at Sturminster Newton, Mr. Savage went to talk to the miller and sort out the sacks of flour. He told Ben that he could sit in the meadow or walk by the river and he would call him when he was ready for him to help lift the sacks on to the cart.

Ben wandered down by the river, enjoying watching the ducks with their ducklings and the many dragonflies skimming along. He started to hum, "All things bright and beautiful" and thought how happy he was. The last few days had been dreadful, but somehow the world seemed a better place again, here by the river in the sunshine.

That was until he saw the man.

Well, Ben wasn't sure it even *was* a man. The gruesome creature looked as if he had been pulled out of a vast lake of fiery-red dye. His hair was red; his face was red; his hands were red; his clothes were red. Only his eyes were a shocking shade of blue and they seemed to pierce right inside Ben, deep inside to all the bad things he had ever done.

Ben screamed. Not just a little scream, but a huge, loud, ear-piercing, terrifyingly terrible scream.

The miller and Mr. Savage came running and even Brownie reared up in fright.

As soon as Ben saw Mr. Savage he ran to him, sobbing. "It's the devil! He's come to get me. I'm sorry, I'm sorry. I shouldn't have stolen those sweets from your jar last year." He felt ashamed of crying because he knew big boys weren't supposed to but he couldn't help it, he was so scared.

Suddenly the miller began to laugh. Then Mr. Savage laughed and then even the "devil" joined in.

"Oh son, sorry you were frightened," said Mr. Savage. "This isn't the devil; it's the raddle man*!"

Hiding behind Mr. Savage, Ben dared to look at the "red" man again. He had never heard of a raddle man and had no idea who he was.

"Sorry," said the raddle man, who spoke in a strange, soft accent. "I didn't mean to scare you. Sometimes I forget I don't look like other men. I collect red ochre from the forest of Dean and bring it to the mills and farms. But it kind of gets inside my skin, see? And it makes me red. I'm a travelling man, a gypsy. I come here now and again to sell raddle to the miller here."

"I need raddle to mark my mill stones," the miller explained to Ben, who was still shaking a little, and would not come out from behind Mr. Savage.

After the miller and the raddle man had gone inside, Ben calmed down, and Mr. Savage took him over to the cart and sat with him in the driving seat. "I brought some of Mrs. Smith's famous dough cake with us as a treat," he said. "Some of the flour is to take back for her. The local mills won't sell to her because she married a German. So I get flour for her and she gives me a bit of dough cake for my trouble. Let's eat it now and have a drink of water and you can tell me properly whatever it was about sweets last year."

Ben felt so bad, he could hardly eat his dough cake, but he swallowed hard, and then tried to explain. "Last year I took a few sweets from a jar on the counter in your shop when you weren't looking. I knew it was wrong, but it seemed … well it seemed thrilling at the time. Afterwards I felt ashamed. I'm really sorry. That's not all, either. I've done and thought and said so many bad things. When I saw the raddle man I thought he was the devil coming to get me."

Mr. Savage was quiet. "It was wrong to steal sweets. But I forgive you and I know you won't do it again. One day, Ben, I hope you will help me in the shop. I am getting older and need a young pair of legs around, and strong arms. I need to be able to trust you, though. I know you are sorry now, but you have to learn to resist temptation. There is a real devil, who is our enemy and tries to tempt us to do wrong, but if we ask Jesus to forgive us and come into our lives, he will help us to live each day in a right way and say 'no' when temptation comes."

"My dad spoke to me a bit like that on Tuesday night before he went away. Lots of things today have made me realise I do need Jesus to help me," Ben said thoughtfully.

"Then, while I finish my payments to the miller, why don't you sit here a little longer and talk to Jesus. He's only a prayer away!" said Mr. Savage, as he climbed off the cart and went back to the mill.

Ben did just that. He quietly spoke his thoughts to Jesus. He asked for forgiveness for all the wrong things he had done which had clogged up his life like weeds in a garden, and asked Jesus to be his friend and to be with him always, helping him to do what was right. It was very quiet. All Ben could hear was Brownie munching her oats and the bees buzzing round the wild flowers, but somehow without hearing any words he felt that Jesus was talking to him. "I love you Ben, and am so glad you want me to be your friend. I will never, ever leave you, whatever happens."

"Down you get, Ben!" called Mr. Savage, arriving back at the cart. "Before we lift the sacks, the miller has something to show you!" Ben jumped down and ran over to the mill. It was hot and dusty inside, and the engine droned as it pumped the watermill that turned the stones to grind the flour.

"Here, son," the miller said. "This is my tin where I keep my raddle. I mark my mill stones with it so that they have the correct grooves. See, it's just a lump of red stuff. But old raddle man mines it and uses it all day and every day, and it never leaves his skin or hair. It dyes everything it touches. He takes it to farmers, too, who use it to mark their sheep. But he's a nice old man and is having his tea now. Come, I have something else to show you. Look up in the eaves there in the engine room. Can you see the swallow's nest? Look carefully – it's a bit dark and the mud nest is well camouflaged. See the babies popping their little heads out? Now isn't that a fantastic sight?"

Ben nodded and smiled. He was thrilled to see the baby swallows poking their heads out of the nest with their beaks wide open. He had never seen such a sight before. This certainly had been a day of adventures!

Mr. Savage and Ben loaded the heavy sacks of flour on to the cart, shook hands with the miller and began the long drive home. The swaying of the cart and the clippety-clop of Brownie's hooves made Ben feel sleepy. As he thought about the day, he knew he had many blessings for which to say thank you, but most of all that Jesus was his friend.

When they stopped near Sherborne for Brownie to have a drink, Mr. Savage suggested to Ben that he climb in the cart and rest against the sacks of flour. Ben did, and when they finally arrived back at Charlestown, Ben was fast asleep! Mr. Savage shook him gently to wake him up. "Come and see me on Saturday morning, Ben, and I'll give you your wages for helping me," he said, as Ben jumped down, said thank you and waved goodbye.

Ben's eyes widened. Wages! For Ben it had been a great outing and adventure. He wasn't expecting any wages!

At home, Mum had already lit the oil lamps and the kettle was on the boil. "Hello Ben, did you have a lovely time? Oh, what's that awful smell?" she asked as Ben came through the door.

"I've brought you a present, Mum," he said with a grin.

She laughed when she saw the bucket of manure. "Oh, not in the house, Ben, take it outside! It's just what I need for the garden, though, thank you! We'll leave it to rot down and next spring it will be perfect to dig into the garden. Don't forget to wash your hands! While you do that, I'll slice the bread for tea, then you must tell me all about your trip."

Two minutes later Ben launched into the events of the day with great enthusiasm. He told his mum all about the things he'd seen on the drive to the mill, about drinking milk straight from the cow and about the baby swallows in their nest. He even told his mum about the raddle man, and how scared he had been, thinking it was the devil. Finally, Ben told his mum that he had asked Jesus to forgive him for all the things he'd done wrong. She gave him a big hug. "It's the best decision you could ever make," she told him.

When they had eaten their bread and had a cup of tea, Ben went to his room and found his New Testament. "I want to read to you from it, like Dad said," he told his mum.

"That would be lovely. I can't read it myself, as I hardly ever went to school," his mum admitted. "Can you read to me about the Good Shepherd? It comes in chapter ten of John's gospel, I think."

Ben found it, and read it aloud to his mum. She sighed. "Isn't it wonderful to know that Jesus is taking care of us, just like a good shepherd takes care of his sheep?" she said. Ben agreed.

"Shall we pray, too, Mum?" After saying the Lord's Prayer together, they prayed for all the members of their family.

"Oh, I almost forgot to tell you," his mum said, just as Ben was heading upstairs to bed. "Two things happened while you were out. First the postman brought a postcard from France. It's from Fred, who is in a place called Albert. That's an easy place to remember since it's the same as your brother's name. He's well and sounds cheerful. The postman kindly read it out for me. Then Sid arrived to play with you. He wants to come round tomorrow morning. I said he could."

"That's great!" said Ben. "Thanks mum! I've got lots to tell him."

Later, Ben lay in bed looking up at the ceiling. He thought about the words he'd read to his mum from the Bible about the Good Shepherd, and Jesus taking care of his sheep, knowing each one by name. He thought about how he had felt Jesus saying to him: "I will never leave you." The words had been a real comfort. And, surprisingly it was a comfort to know Jesus knew everything about him – even the horrible, nasty, selfish and mean things. Ben sighed peacefully, turned over and went straight to sleep.

Chapter Ten

On Friday morning Ben was so glad to see Sid again. He showed him the postcard that Fred had sent from France. He had promised to do some digging in the garden, ready to sow more vegetables, so Sid helped him and as they worked he told him all about the adventure of going to Sturminster mill.

"I wish I could have come with you," sighed Sid. "Mum needs so much help at the moment she won't let us go out much. I love my brothers and sisters, but they can be a pain to look after sometimes. Mum's told us there will be another baby in September. We're such a big family already: that will make us twelve children altogether!"

"Do you think your mum would let you and Vera come out tomorrow afternoon? We need to find this tunnel over at Radipole churchyard. Mum has asked me to go over to Radipole anyway to show Molly the postcard from Fred and to tell her about Mum's job. Molly won't be coming home as usual on Sunday as she's already had a day off."

Sid nodded. "That would be great! I do hope my mum says yes. Can't you come in the morning? We'd have all day, then."

"I have promised to help Mr. Savage on Saturday mornings."

"Oh. Couldn't we go this afternoon, then, when you've finished the digging? It won't take long now I'm helping you!"

"Good idea," agreed Ben. "I'll ask mum. It will depend if she's got anything else she wants me to do. I promised dad I would be the man of the house while he is away. I really miss him already, and Albert. I never thought it would be lonely to have your own bedroom, but it is. I even miss his snoring!"

Sid laughed out loud. "If you miss snoring, you want to come and stay at our house!"

Ben's mum agreed that he could go that afternoon, as did Sid and Vera's mum, so it was a delighted trio who set off to Radipole, enjoying the walk down the lanes in the shade of the trees. Ben had his catapult and stones in his pocket, in case he had the chance to catch some more rabbits.

When Sid, Vera and Ben arrived at Radipole Manor, Cook recognised them at once and cheerfully invited them into the kitchen. She gave them homemade lemonade and biscuits while she went to find Molly. They were really glad of the drink and they savoured every mouthful of the delicious biscuits. After they had delivered the postcard and the message telling Molly about her mum's new job, Ben told Cook they were going to the churchyard to try and catch some rabbits for dinner.

"When you've done that, call in before you go home,"

said Cook. "I can't let you go home without another drink in this hot weather!"

"Thank you," said the children, grinning at each other.

"The cook is such a nice lady," remarked Vera, as they headed for the churchyard. "When I leave school I hope I have a lovely place like that to work in."

Ben needed quiet to catch rabbits, so they agreed that while Ben went to the churchyard on the other side of the road to hunt for rabbits, Sid and Vera would stay on the side by the church, and look for tunnels. Some of the tombstones nearest the church were very old. Most were covered in moss, and some were leaning sideways. Others were covered with brambles and stinging nettles. She wasn't sure why, but something about the place gave Vera the creeps. She was glad she had Sid with her. He might only be an hour older than she was, but she felt safe with him.

"We must come in September and pick the blackberries," said Vera, looking at all the blackberry bushes. "There will be hundreds here!"

"There are hundreds of nettles now!" a voice from behind them suddenly said. Sid and Vera nearly jumped out of their skin, but it was only David, the footman from Radipole House, who had driven them home on their last visit. He had a huge basket and shears and was gathering nettles. This time he wasn't in his smart uniform, but just ordinary shirt and trousers. He smiled at them.

"Did you know that nettles make very good soup?" he said. "Cook wants some. You could gather some to take home for your mum if you like! I'm sure Cook would give you the recipe. Her Ladyship wants me to tidy up the churchyard a bit while I'm here. Everything's so overgrown. It's been neglected since the war began. The sexton* who used to look after it has been called up. I didn't think I'd like working in a graveyard, but there's a lot of history here. Did you know there is a secret tunnel running from the church to the house?"

Sid and Vera stared at him with their mouths open. "Is there really?" asked Sid. "Can we see it? We'd really, really love to see a secret tunnel!"

"Why not?" said David. "Tell you what, I'll finish filling this basket for Cook, then we can take it back to the house through the tunnel. But remember, it's a secret tunnel and secrets have to be kept!"

"Oh," said Vera. "But Ben's on the other side of the road catching rabbits. Please can he be part of the secret, too?"

"Yes, of course," David smiled, "but don't go telling the whole world! You go over and get Ben while I cut these nettles. You could pick a few fresh, small dandelion leaves for Cook, too, if you like! She'd be pleased with those for her salad. Watch out for the sap though, or it'll stain your clothes, then you'll be in your mums' bad books!"

Sid and Vera couldn't wait to tell Ben the news about the tunnel. They ran across the road to find him, and to their amazement saw that he had already caught three rabbits. Ben had tied their feet together with string so he could carry them.

"I'm getting better at this," he said. "You can have two for your family." His eyes grew round as his friends told him about the tunnel. "Now the Peppermint Detective Agency will solve the mystery for sure," he said, "only I don't have any peppermints left for us to suck!"

They laughed together and ran back to the church where David was waiting in the porch. As they went inside Ben thought how much had happened in the few days since he had sat there and said a prayer.

David led them to the pulpit. The steps up into the pulpit were stone, but he gently moved the bottom step and underneath there was a trap door, which he pulled open. Ben gasped. "Wow, it's well hidden!"

"Was it a pirate's tunnel?" asked Sid. "The ships used to come right up the River Wey to Radipole in the olden days, didn't they?"

"To be honest with you, no one really knows what the tunnel was used for," replied David. "It might have been used by pirates and smugglers. On the other hand, because the church and house are so old, it may have been used as a way for the priest to escape and hide at the time when the priests were being hunted down. I'm not very good at history, but I did hear His Lordship say it was very old. He showed the tunnel to me before he went away to fight. Anyway, lower yourselves carefully through the hole after me. I'll go first and help you down. It's pretty dark so stay there until I've lit a candle."

Sid went down first after David, then Vera, followed by Ben. It was chilly down in the tunnel, and Ben shivered. He held his nose, too, as a dank, stale smell hit him. The trap door had let them into what appeared to be a large, dark cave, completely underground. David put the trap door into place and pulled another large stone, which made a grating sound.

"That's a very clever mechanism which puts the stair back into place, so no one knows we are down here." David told them.

Just as the darkness completely closed in, they heard a scuttling noise, and Vera screamed. David patted her shoulder. "Don't worry, the scuttling was just a mouse. It won't hurt you. It probably smelt Ben's rabbits! Is everyone ready? I'll lead the way with the candle. Vera, if you follow me, then the boys can bring up the rear. Watch your step because the floor is uneven and a bit slippery in places where there's moss."

The friends were intrigued, excited and a bit scared – all at the same time, and began to follow David through the narrow passage. David had to stoop because he was quite tall, but the children could stand upright. It took about five minutes or so for them to get to the house. David carried the candle, Vera carried the basket of nettles and Ben carried the rabbits.

"Look out for anything to do with a spy," Ben

whispered to his friends, and they nodded. They all kept a good eye open but were a little disappointed because they didn't see any evidence of a spy's lair. However, Ben noticed what seemed to be a place where once another tunnel might have led off the one they were in. The wall looked as if it had been blocked off with stones. He couldn't be sure, but made a mental note to tell the others when they were alone.

They wondered where they would emerge: maybe in the kitchen? Or perhaps the cellar? In fact, the tunnel ended quite suddenly. David once again pushed a stone in the wall and a flagstone moved. "Wow, that's bright!" said Ben, as dazzling light flooded the tunnel.

"That's what happens when your eyes get used to the dark," said David with a smile. "Here, up the ladder you go!" He pointed out a rope ladder and took the basket from Vera while she climbed out. The others followed her, helping pass the basket and the rabbits up. Then David blew out the candle, put it carefully on a ledge, and climbed out himself. He pressed another mechanism on the wall that moved the flagstone back into place.

"It's amazing!" Ben remarked, looking round at where they were.

"It is," agreed David. "To think it works so well, even all these hundreds of years later!"

"So where are we?" asked Sid.

"We're in one of the old stables," said David. "When the tunnel was made, the stables would have been an amazing escape route. You could either ride away on one of the horses, or go and hide in the house. We only have a couple of horses to stable now, so His Lordship keeps his motor car here."

Sid and Ben rushed over to have a look. Ben wanted to feel how smooth the silky bonnet was, but was afraid of putting any fingerprints on the shiny surface. "How fast can it go?" he asked.

"They say she can reach speeds of 50 miles per hour but there's a speed restriction of 20. You have to coax her around the bends especially if the road is wet," David replied.

"Are there any other tunnels in the house?" asked Vera. "Or anywhere else round here?"

"Not as far as I know," answered David, "but in the library, which is all wood panelled, there is a secret room behind one panel. We think that was a hiding place for a priest. It might have been for stolen goods, too, as years ago the gentry were often involved in smuggling. I can't show you that without the master's permission, and I don't know if he'll come home on leave before this war ends."

"Well, thanks so much for bringing us through the tunnel," said Ben.

Sid nodded in agreement. "It's the most exciting thing that has ever happened to me!"

As they were walking across the courtyard back to the house, Ben remembered about the ghost Cook had told them about. "David, Cook told us there's a ghost living round here. Have you ever seen it?"

"Only once. I had gone down to lock the church after the choir practice ended and I saw a figure all bent over, wearing a long black robe with a hood covering his face. I tell you, the hairs on the back of my neck stood up. I couldn't get away quickly enough!"

Back in the cosy kitchen, Cook had a pot of tea ready for them. She had baked scones, too, and they were buttered and had a thick layer of jam spread on them. "It's so nice to have someone to spoil again," she said with a smile. "This big house is too quiet with all the men gone to war. Thank goodness we still have David."

He handed her the basket of nettles and dandelion leaves with a sigh. "I just wish I could enlist. I get so fed up when people look at me as if I were a coward. I've even been given white feathers. I feel so ashamed."

"It's not your fault that you had polio when you were young! You can't help your limp and your bad chest. Anyway, you are a great blessing to us, and never forget that! Oh, we've had some news while you were out," continued Cook. "The mistress says we may have wounded soldiers staying here. The house will be like a hospital to help them get better. That will keep us all busy. I think your Molly fancies herself as a volunteer nurse already!"

"We have a camp for wounded Australian soldiers in Chickerell," said Ben. "Sometimes the soldiers come to church on Sunday. We see them in the village and they are always friendly. Mum always says we should be kind and smile at them because they are so far from home.

It's too far for them to be sent back to Australia to recover."

"Talking about being far from home, it's time you children were on your way," said Cook. "Your mothers will be worrying!" Cook looked at David. "Why don't you take the children home in the horse and cart? I'm sure Her Ladyship won't mind. Then they can take some scones home, too."

The children jumped up and down in delight. Another ride in the cart! And scones to take home! It had been another amazing day in what had become such an amazing week.

"School is going to be really boring after this!" Ben said to Sid, as they climbed up into the cart.

Sid grinned back. "Maybe the Belgian Flush epidemic will continue!"

Chapter Eleven

After the weekend, life got so busy for Ben that he didn't have time to do anything about the bottle for a long time. School opened again, and the teachers made all the pupils work extra hard to catch up, because exams were coming up.

Also, Ben's mum began working in the factory making ammunition. She had to leave early in the morning and came home well after Ben had returned from school. She always seemed to be tired, so Ben had to work really hard to do all the jobs in the house and garden.

He noted with alarm that the whites of her eyes soon turned a bit yellow. He did as much as he could at home to help, but still he worried. What if she turned completely yellow, just like the raddle man had turned red? He knew that some workers in the factory had become ill after a very short time working there; a few had even died. He wished she would give up the job, but she insisted that she was fine and the money was needed.

Ben still read the New Testament and prayed with his mum before going to bed, but on his own, in his bedroom, he begged Jesus to get his mum out of the factory. He was so afraid she might die.

Before he sailed to France, Ben's dad was allowed a weekend's leave. Ben was so pleased to see him! The training had been hard. Ben thought his dad looked really smart and handsome in his uniform, but he seemed older somehow.

It was a really special weekend because Albert was also able to come home on leave, too. After dinner on the Friday, all the family sat around the table, talking. Albert was really enjoying his training and kept them all entertained with stories about driving the tanks and making new friends. "I tell you, there won't be a war by the time I get to the front line in September," he said cheerily.

Ben really hoped and prayed he would be right.

Molly told them all about Radipole Manor being transformed into a hospital for wounded soldiers. Already she had applied to be a V.A.D.* nurse and was reading nursing books in her spare time. She had brought some bandages with her and practised on Ben! She wanted him to be her patient, but he wasn't very patient at all and ended up getting very cross with her. He would so much rather be playing outside!

"Your turn now, Ben," his dad said, after Molly had finished her news. "What are you up to?"

"Well, Dad, you'll never believe this! Mr. Savage has given me a job as his Saturday delivery boy. He managed to find a bike with a metal cage on the front, where you can put packages. I couldn't reach the pedals though, even with the saddle at its lowest, so Mr. Savage fixed large wooden blocks on each pedal. It took me a few days to learn to ride it, but now I can whizz along!"

"Well done, Ben," said Albert, with a whistle. "With me in a tank and you on your bike we'll win the war!" Everyone laughed.

"I begin at eight-thirty and finish at one-thirty," Ben went on. "Mr. Savage has most of the deliveries ready, but sometimes I help him make up the orders. I haven't made a mistake yet, though I have fallen off the bike a few times. I earn sixpence a week, and a pennyworth of peppermints! I give my wages to mum. I really am the man of the house now!"

"Well done, son," said his father. "I knew I could trust you to take care of everything while I'm away. I hope your school work isn't suffering, though. I still have dreams that you won't have to leave school at fourteen, like I did."

"I'm getting good marks for spellings and tables and mental arithmetic every week, but Vera is always top of the class. I'm usually about fourth or fifth. It's a shame because Vera wants to be a teacher, but she has to leave school as soon as she can to help her mum at home."

On Sunday evening, after Albert had returned to Bovington Barracks and Molly to Radipole, Ben and his dad had a short walk down to the Fleet.

"Dad, I miss you," said Ben with a sigh. "So much has happened since you went away. I want to tell you that Jesus is my Saviour and friend. I talk to Him every day as well as reading the New Testament you gave me. Mum and I also read and pray each evening, though recently she is so tired. I worry about her turning yellow."

"So do I, Ben. But we have to let her make her own choices, and she wants to help win the war, just like us. Let's keep praying for her to stay well. I'm thrilled to hear your news. That makes me very happy. Never forget you are not an accident. You're a very special person and God has a special plan for you."

"I won't forget." He paused. "And I pray for you every day, Dad. I love you so much!" He hugged his dad tightly.

Next morning it was so hard to say goodbye. As Ben hugged his dad, he felt a big lump in his throat. He tried very hard not to cry. In the back of his mind was this awful dread that he might never see his dad again.

When he had gone, his mum made him sit down and eat some breakfast before she went to work and he went to school.

"I couldn't tell you till your dad had gone because it's a surprise," she said, "but Molly is taking you to London on Wednesday to wave your dad off on the troop train to France! I know you can get time off school for that. She has written a note for you to take with you this morning." His mum put her hand in her apron and produced a note for him to give to the head teacher. "I wish I could come, but I have to be at work. If we don't make the bombs and shells for our soldiers, then they can't win the war, can they?"

Ben could hardly believe it! He was going to London! He had never been that far before. In fact, the furthest he had ever been was Sturminster mill! He had heard about London, of course, and seen a few pictures in a book at school. Would he see Big Ben, the Houses of Parliament, or Buckingham Palace where the King lived? It was almost too exciting to think about! And then he realised that in order to get there he would have to go on a train. He had always thought how exciting it would be to travel on a train! It was really kind of Molly to take him.

"Thank you, Jesus," Ben said in his mind. "Thank you for my family. Please keep them all safe."

Then he ran to school, the note firmly tucked into his trouser pocket. Sid and Vera were waiting for him at the gate as they usually did. They thought he would be feeling sad after seeing his dad off to the war, so were amazed to see him grinning! He explained to them about Molly taking him to London on Wednesday. "I can't believe you're going on a train!" said Sid enviously.

After the register was taken, Ben gave his note to his teacher. He found it hard to concentrate on his lessons that morning. At dinner time the headmaster called him into his office and gave him permission to go to London. "You will have to tell us all about it," the headmaster added with a smile, as Ben was leaving.

When school was over Ben ran into Mr. Savage's shop

before going home. "I've got such exciting news!" he told him. "I'm going up to London on Wednesday to wave my dad off to the front!"

"Goodness me, that will be an adventure!" said Mr. Savage. "I went there once, many years ago. I was young then, and found it all very exciting. Be careful though; it's not like here. Even when I was young, there were so many horses, carts and carriages it was difficult to cross the road. I can't imagine what it will be like now, with motor cars and bicycles, too. I went for Queen Victoria's Diamond Jubilee – that's how long ago it was! Anyway, somewhere upstairs in the flat I have a box of special things. I am sure I still have a Union Jack. Come in after school tomorrow Ben, and if I can find it you can have it to wave goodbye to your dad. He's a very brave man and will be doing a very dangerous job."

"Thanks," said Ben. "I'll see you tomorrow." Ben soon caught up with Sid and Vera who were walking home with some of their younger brothers and sisters. It took them ages to get back: the smaller children were tired and it was a long way.

They chatted as they walked along together. "We've not done anything more about looking for another tunnel," said Vera. "Mum needs lots of help with the cooking and cleaning because she's so tired with another baby coming soon. She's already told me that I can't come to school every day any more. She says the school authorities will turn a blind eye if I stay at home to help. But I don't want them to! I really love school!"

Ben nodded. "I know. I've been thinking about the poem clues, too. The tunnel in the poem is definitely in the churchyard, not the church, like the one David showed us. I think we ought to try to find it as soon as we can. If we can't solve the riddle we should take the message to someone else, like the police."

"You're right," agreed Sid and they both sighed. Ben was troubled because the days were going by and they were no closer to catching the spy. They had been making such good progress but things had come to a bit of a standstill now they were all so busy.

The children reached the top of the lane that led to Ben's house. How he wished he could have invited them in to play, but he knew he had to fetch some wood, make up the fire in the stove, look after the garden, prepare the dinner and then try to catch some rabbits for tomorrow's meal. He couldn't go away on Wednesday unless everything was done. His mum was too tired these days, and the yellow was spreading all over her face and arms.

Ben continued to be worried about his mum – but was glad he could pray about it all. It was such a comfort that Jesus had whispered to him that he would never leave him.

Sometimes Ben feared for all his family, though: that dad, mum, Fred and Albert would all die. Then he would end up in the workhouse. He hated this war. Would it ever end? It had already been two years since it all began and he knew that it wasn't going very well for the Allies*. Each day there was news of more and more young men being injured or killed. Closer to home the camp in Chickerell was almost full to the brim with wounded Australian soldiers all trying to get better and return to the war. Soon there would be more wounded soldiers in Radipole Manor … so many injuries.

Ben sighed and started on his first task: fetching wood. As he worked, Ben wondered what his sister would look like in a nurse's uniform. He guessed she would look very smart!

Chapter Twelve

On Wednesday Ben was up with the lark before it was light. He splashed cold water over his face and dressed in his Sunday best clothes. His mum had given him his train fare. She had saved it out of some of his wages. He had the flag Mr. Savage had given him along with a huge bag of peppermints – much more than a pennyworth! Mum had made him a cup of tea and given him a hunk of bread. She hugged him and hoped he would have a wonderful day. He ran up the lane to wait for Molly.

Molly arrived, driven in the pony and trap by David. They both looked very smart. Molly was wearing a pretty summer dress and a matching hat and gloves, and even though David wasn't in his livery, he looked as if he was going somewhere special.

"Jump up Ben, we're going to catch the milk train* to London," said Molly brightly. "David's coming with us, to make sure we don't get lost in the big city."

"That's right," said David. "I am taking care of Molly. You might as well know that I am walking out with her. She's a wonderful girl, is your sister."

Molly went bright pink and giggled. "Oh, don't,

David, I'm no one special, just Molly Goodenough!"

"You're special to me and certainly good enough!" quipped David. Ben liked David, but was a bit embarrassed, and hoped they weren't going to be soppy all day.

"What's going to happen to the pony while we are in London?" he asked, changing the subject.

"A friend of mine is meeting us at Weymouth station," replied David. "He's going to use the pony and trap for the day, then he will bring it to meet us off the last train. Her Ladyship has been so kind, letting us use her pony and trap. She said things will be very different when the house becomes a hospital, so we might as well have a bit of enjoyment while we can!"

Everything went to plan and soon the three of them were settled on the train. It was thrilling to actually ride on a train – a first for all of them. They had a whole carriage to themselves for most of the journey. Outside the carriage was a corridor and at the end of that was a toilet. Ben, Molly and David thought it was such a novelty to use an inside toilet* that they each went to visit it in turn!

The engine hissed as it pulled out of Weymouth and headed towards Dorchester. Ben thought it was like being inside a big iron dragon that was running to London! The train lurched a little from side to side and he wobbled when he tried to get up and walk. He soon got used to the motion, though. The first stop was Radipole Halt. "We could have got on here!" Molly remarked. Then it steamed through the hill to Upwey, and stopped at every little station in order to collect the milk churns from the farms.

In spite of all the excitement, Ben fell asleep to the rhythm of the train clicking on the rails. When he woke up, for a few moments he couldn't think where he was. Then he remembered! By now the train was going through town after town. David explained they were getting close to London.

Ben squeezed his face against the window so that he didn't miss seeing anything. He wanted to open the window, but the guard had warned him about sooty smuts getting into his eyes and on to his clothes. He might get in trouble if he spoiled his best clothes!

Finally the train arrived at Waterloo Station. Ben was glad that he had been warned about the traffic. It was so busy and so noisy. He couldn't hear very well when Molly spoke to him. Molly was holding David's hand tightly, and Ben was holding Molly's other hand, even though he felt a bit silly. He was frightened of getting lost. The people around him were speaking English, but it sounded very weird to him.

"Why can't I understand what people are saying?" he asked David.

"Many people in London speak cockney* English, but they also have their own language where they use rhyming words like 'apples and pears' when they mean 'stairs'. Sometimes they spell words backwards, too."

Ben thought that was all very confusing. Why did

they need to speak differently? Maybe they didn't want other people to understand – a bit like spies using a code.

Although David hadn't been to London before, Lady Worthington had given him instructions about getting to places, and given him a map. He took charge of Molly and Ben and that gave them confidence. First, they had to make their way to Victoria Station to see their father's regiment leave. They took a horse-drawn bus and Ben marvelled at the busy city and all the buildings they passed on the way. They got off near Victoria Station and looked for a café where they could get something to eat, because they were a bit early.

Ben had never eaten in a proper café before. He felt very grand and grown up and the food tasted very good.

When they walked into the station forecourt, Ben looked around in amazement. It was teeming with people. Not only soldiers, but hundreds of women and children, who had all come to wave goodbye to their loved ones.

"How will we ever find Dad? There are soldiers everywhere!" Ben cried in dismay. David pointed out to him certain points where men were gathering to join their regiments.

"We just have to look for the Dorsetshire regimental flag and drummers. That way we will find your Dad. Private* Goodenough, he'll be called now!"

Actually, it didn't take too long, because just as they made out the regiment's flag, their dad spotted them, and gave a whoop of surprise and joy! “My Moll and Ben! I didn’t expect to see you!” he said in delight. “And who is this young man with you?” he asked Molly, raising his eyebrows.

When she had hugged and kissed her father, she introduced him to David. “We’ve just started walking out together, Dad. You weren’t around to ask permission, but we hope you approve.”

“As long as David takes good care of you and treats you like a lady, you have my blessing,” he replied. David beamed at Molly and squeezed her hand. Ben tried not to look.

Soon the regiment had to board the train. Ben gave his dad one last, long hug, then as his dad stepped on to the train, he pushed his big bag of peppermints into his hand. “Oh, thanks, son,” his dad said in surprise, peering into the bag. “Peppermints! I shall really enjoy these!”

After final goodbyes and a lot of waving, their dad moved away down the train. Molly cried, and David put his arm around her. The guard blew his whistle. The train hissed loudly, then the wheels began to slowly turn. It was on its way! There was no turning back now. Soon, the soldiers would be in Belgium and France, facing the enemy. Along with a whole crowd of women and children, Ben waved and waved his Union Jack until the train was out of sight and his arm ached. “Please be with Dad and keep him safe,” he prayed silently.

Once the train had gone, David got out his map. He wanted to cheer Molly and Ben up. "We have lots of time left, so let's do some sightseeing. I'd like to go on one of these new-fangled trains which run under the ground. How about it?"

"Oh yes, please!" said Ben, and Molly nodded her head. They made their way to the underground railway. There were no escalators then, so it meant lots of stairs to go down to reach the platform. It wasn't long before a train arrived for Westminster.

"Now, Her Ladyship says from here it is just a short walk to see the Abbey, the Houses of Parliament, Big Ben and Old Father Thames from Westminster Bridge," David told them when they had got back up to street level. "So let's go!"

"Can we go to Buckingham Palace after that?" asked Molly. "I'd love to see where the King lives."

"Yes, it's next on the list!" answered David with a big smile. "Your wish is my desire!" Molly giggled.

Ben decided he liked London. It was amazing! He wished he had a camera, like the man taking photos of the goods train, so that he could take photographs to show Sid and Vera. As it was, he tried to memorise all he saw so that he could tell them about it later. There was so much to take in! It seemed strange to be in a place full of roads and traffic of all sorts, and not to see any fields, or even gardens! The buildings were huge, and Ben was amazed when he saw how wide the river Thames was. Standing on Westminster Bridge and looking down at it made him feel a bit dizzy.

After a while the trio began to get hungry again and bought some muffins from a muffin man's stall and munched them as they walked along.

They were also feeling a bit worn out. London seemed hot and tiring after the leafy lanes and sea breezes of Dorset. "Let's catch a bus again and go to the Tower of London," suggested David. "We have plenty of time to do that before we go back to Waterloo Station for the train home." As they waited at the bus stop, Ben watched the horses pulling the buses up and down the road. It made him think of Brownie. He was glad his favourite horse didn't have to work in London. He didn't think he would like the noise and the bustle of traffic.

"I'm glad we haven't got to leave till the last train, even though I'm tired," remarked Ben. "There's so much to see."

"Well, we have no choice, love," answered Molly. "The government have taken over the trains and most of them are used for troops, so we're only allowed to travel on the first and the last trains."

When they reached the Tower, they got off the bus and stood to admire it from the outside. "It's still used for prisoners," David told Ben. "It's where they put German spies."

As David was speaking, they heard a very strange droning noise coming from the sky. Everyone around them looked up and gasped. There above them was a Zeppelin airship*! It was huge. Ben's mouth dropped open and his eyes widened. He had heard about Zeppelins, but London had been their main target and none had been seen in their part of Dorset. For a few seconds, all three of them stood looking at the huge, sausage-shaped object with the cabin underneath. Ben was sure he could see people in it; Germans who were intent on dropping bombs on them.

Suddenly they heard ships' hooters blaring from the docks, and saw policemen on bikes blowing whistles as people ran for cover. "I thought the Zeppelins only came in the evening!" exclaimed David in terror, clutching Molly's hand. "It's not even getting dark yet."

The street was in chaos. People were running in all directions, looking afraid and confused. Ben saw a man scoop up his toddler and dash for cover. The child was howling in fear. Several men with loud speakers tried to bring order: "Don't run! Please walk quietly to a place of safety!" But the crowd ignored them. They just wanted to run away from the Zeppelins as fast as they could, before the bombs dropped.

David, Molly and Ben all ran together, propelled along by the crowd, who seemed to be making their way to shelter under the railway arches at nearby Fenchurch Street Station.

Ben was terrified as he heard bombs explode and smelled the smoke from buildings set on fire. He crouched on the ground under one of the railway arches with his arms over his head and his eyes tight shut. He thought he was going to be crushed by all the people around him. When the noise of the bombing stopped, he stood up a little shakily. He found himself squashed against the side of a railway arch by a huge crowd of people. With a feeling of horror, he realised he couldn't see either Molly or David. Panicking, he tried to move. But he couldn't, there were too many people all round him. He tried to call out Molly's name, but he was so terrified nothing came out of his mouth.

"Will we all die?" he wondered. "Jesus, help us!" he cried out silently.

"I will never, ever leave you," a quiet voice inside him said. It calmed Ben.

"You alone then, Ducks?" someone asked Ben in the unfamiliar cockney accent. It was a rather large lady. She seemed to be clucking rather like a mother duck herself!

Ben managed to find his voice, and in his very West Country accent replied, "I seem to have lost my sister and David. And we have to catch a train back home soon." He felt like crying because it was all so frightening. There was such a lot of noise from fire engines, ambulances and policemen rushing around. The smoke was making it hard to see what was happening. He realised again how very terrible war was. People got hurt and killed.

"That Zepp must 'ave bin goin' for the docks, I reckon." said the lady kindly. "Very soon you'll 'ear the 'all clear' sound, and people will go 'ome. If yer can't find yer sister then, I'll take yer to the Bobby shop*. Don't worry, yer'll be alright." With that the woman fished around in her basket and handed Ben a currant bun. "I've bin to the market. 'Ave a bun, Ducks. It's a tiddly bit stale but is still good to eat."

Ben thanked her. He was glad for something to do, and for being next to the kind woman. He nibbled at the bun, making it last as long as possible. He wondered what on earth a "Bobby shop" was, but decided not to ask. He knew God was with him and would look after him. Maybe He had even sent this woman with the bun to help him!

Sure enough, before too long the all-clear siren sounded and people were shouting, "All clear, thank God!" as they began to leave the arches. Then to his great relief he saw Molly and David. Molly was crying and David was looking very worried. They were calling his name.

"Looks like you've bin found!" said the plump lady, with a smile. Ben nodded and ran to Molly, almost hugging the life out of her. Then he remembered his manners and turned round to thank the lady, but she had disappeared into the crowd.

All three of them were shaken by the Zeppelin raid. They looked dirty and bedraggled from the smoke and from being crushed in the crowd. Still, none of that mattered. They were just glad to be safe.

They had to walk a long way before they found a bus to take them back to Waterloo Station. Fortunately, their train was still scheduled to run on time. Wearily they climbed on board. For a while they talked together about the raid, and how awful life must be for the people of London. The Germans were killing so many people with these Zeppelin raids and no one seemed to be able to shoot the airships down*. It made Ben even more proud of the fact that his dad and Fred had gone to fight the Germans, and soon Albert would join them. He was doing his bit too, by hunting rabbits!

After a while they all nodded off, exhausted from their eventful day. It was a good job that Weymouth was the last station of the line, because they were deeply asleep when the engine stopped and the guard called out, "Train terminates here!"

Chapter Thirteen

Ben found it hard to get up for school the following day. After assembly, which he yawned all the way through, his class teacher wanted him to tell everyone about his visit to London. It was all still so fresh in Ben's mind – especially the fright of the Zeppelin raid – that it was easy for him to talk about it all.

He stood at the front of the class and told everyone about seeing his father off to war at Victoria Station; all the sights of London; the traffic and the people who spoke so differently from them, and then the terror of the raid. The class seemed to think he was some sort of hero, but Ben knew he wasn't: he had been scared almost to death! He suddenly felt he should say something about Jesus being with him. His classmates might laugh at him, but he was sure that God had sent the plump lady to help him.

Actually, nobody laughed. The teacher said it was a miracle, and the lady could have been an angel, because angels came in all shapes and sizes. The teacher encouraged his class to remember that Jesus always heard their prayers. After that he led them in prayers for the people of London and other big cities who were suffering from Zeppelin raids, as well as for their family members and friends who were away, fighting in the war.

After school, Sid, Vera and Ben talked together. "It could happen here," said Vera. "A Zeppelin raid, I mean. If that man on the bike was really a spy, then they could come and bomb the naval dockyard in Portland Harbour, the Whitehead's torpedo works, Portland Castle where they store ammunition, and the Verne Fortress. There are lots of targets around here."

For a moment they all stood in silence. It was a horrible thought, but what Vera had said was true; the fighting could come to Weymouth and Portland. The Germans might even bomb Sid and Vera's dad or Ben's mum, while they were at work.

"We have to find that tunnel in case there is a spy living there," said Ben at last. "We just have to. I had a thought the other day. You looked on the church side of the churchyard, but I was catching rabbits on the school side. We need to search there, too."

"Yes, and we need to do it soon," agreed Sid. "Maybe we could do that instead of going to the Sunday School treat. That's next Wednesday, and school closes for it, so we would be free."

Vera's face fell. "Oh don't let's do that," she said. "Don't forget we're supposed to being taking the little 'uns to the treat. It's one of the best days of the year!"

"That's true," agreed Ben with a sigh. "The vicar arranges so many fun games for us and we have a smashing tea! We would be missed and questions asked, too. Maybe we can go over to Radipole on Saturday afternoon after I've finished work?"

The Peppermint Detectives agreed on this. They really wanted to solve the mystery of the message in the bottle: it was so annoying how things just kept getting in the way!

Although Ben was enjoying helping Mr. Savage and earning some money and was also now very good at catching rabbits, he was becoming increasingly worried about his mum. She seemed to be turning a deeper shade of yellow every day. She was always tired from working long shifts and then doing the housework, although he tried to do all he could to help. Ben noticed she did a lot of coughing at night, too. It played on his mind.

Two weeks after he had been to London, Ben was asked to go to the headmaster's office during class. Everyone looked at him with dread. When that happened it was usually bad family news. With a sinking feeling in his heart, Ben knocked on the headmaster's door. "Come in," came the answer, and Ben opened the door to see his mum sitting with the headmaster. He knew something was really wrong. Was it Fred or his dad? His heart was racing.

The headmaster smiled at him kindly. "Sit down, Ben." Ben sat on the chair next to his mum, who reached out her hand to hold his. "Your mother received a letter from the War Office this morning," the headmaster told him. "It's not very good news, I'm afraid. There was a terrible explosion in the trenches above where your father was working, and he is reported missing. The War Office doesn't give many details. There may be a possibility that his body will be found and you will be informed and his personal things sent home. It could be that he is alive and has been taken to a field hospital. Sometimes it takes a while for the names to be released. He could even have been taken prisoner, but that seems a little unlikely. I am so sorry, son. Waiting for news and not knowing what has happened is almost worse than hearing about your loved one's death. However, don't give up hope. It does say 'missing', not 'dead'. Now, the vicar is on his way to take you and your mother home. You can have the rest of the day off."

Ben was reeling from the shock. He looked at his Mum. She was trying not to cry. A lump came to his throat, but he was determined to be brave. Maybe his dad would soon be found. He couldn't imagine life without him.

The school secretary brought in some tea, and they drank it while they waited for the vicar to come. She and the headmaster were very kind and sympathetic, but that made it even harder not to cry. They went into the church with the vicar, who prayed with them before he took them home.

Ben's mum had also been told not to go to work for the rest of that day. It was awful at home. Both of them cried and didn't know how to comfort each other.

After making a big pot of tea, Mum suddenly put her

face in her hands. "Oh my goodness me! I need to tell Molly," she said to Ben. "I forgot all about letting her and Albert know. And how do we let Fred know?"

Ben thought for a minute. "Mum, I can go to Mr. Savage and ask him if I can borrow the delivery bike to cycle over to Radipole. That would be the quickest way to tell Molly. She and David will know how to get to Albert and tell him. I expect the vicar will know how to contact Fred's regiment. Why don't you walk up to Chickerell with me and you can go to the vicarage and I'll go to the shop?"

"Brilliant idea, Ben! Yes, that's what we'll do. What a blessing you are to me!" said his mum, smiling for the first time since she heard the news. After giving Ben a quick hug, they both got ready and walked to the village. Mr. Savage was shocked at the terrible news and was only too pleased to help. Soon Ben was on the way to Radipole, cycling as fast as he could. He was breathless when he arrived at the manor. As usual it was the cook who opened the door.

"Whatever has happened, Ben?" she said, shocked at the sight of him, breathless and sweating.

"I have bad news for Molly," he blurted out, trying not to cry again.

Molly came running when she was called, and burst into tears when she heard about her dad. Cook comforted her and went to fetch Lady Worthington and David. They came into the kitchen and Ben told them what had happened.

"I promised Mum that I would ask you to think how we could let our Albert know the news," Ben told them. "I thought you would know what to do."

David looked at Lady Worthington. "Could I drive the trap over to Bovington now, Ma'am? It's about ten miles."

"Yes, of course David! And Molly must go with you."

Ben was so grateful that David had known what to do. He left the manor house with a slightly lighter heart. He pushed his bike down the front path and through the gate. By now the school children had all left the school and the teacher had locked the gate. Ben was just getting on his bike when he heard a rustling in the bushes just behind the lavatories. He stopped, suddenly remembering about the tunnel. If the Germans had killed or injured his dad, then he was jolly well going to catch that spy. A sudden surge of anger rose up in him, almost making him feel sick. Leaving his bike by the gate he crept into the churchyard.

There was a wall between the school buildings and the cemetery. Quietly he listened. There was no rustling now but Ben heard a distinct grating noise. It reminded him of something which at first he couldn't place. Then all at once it came to him! It was like the noise of the mechanism of the secret tunnel in the church. He was sure he now knew where the spy's tunnel was!

For a moment he was uncertain what to do. It was very tempting to stop and investigate, but the sounds probably meant the spy had returned to his base. And he couldn't tackle a spy on his own: he needed reinforcements. He decided to come back with Sid and Vera. Together they would flush this spy out!

His anger seemed to give him extra energy as he cycled back to Chickerell. When he took the bike back to Mr. Savage he found the shop full of Australian troops who had been injured and were now recovering. Somehow seeing these men, several of whom were on crutches, made Ben even more determined to catch that spy.

His mum was glad to see him back safely, and to know that Molly and David were going to contact Albert. The vicar had been very kind and promised to go to the headquarters of the Dorsetshire Regiment, in Dorchester. They would send the news on to Fred in France.

Ben and his mum were both worn out by all the sadness and worry of the day. Neither felt like eating any supper, so they just made a cup of tea. Before they turned in for the night Ben found his little New Testament.

"I thought that the Zeppelin raid was the most terrible thing that has ever happened to me, but today has been even worse," he said to his mum. "Shall we read the Bible and say our prayers?"

"Yes, Ben, let's do that," said his mum with a sigh. "Perhaps we will find some comfort from God's word." There was a bookmark in the place where they had reached, because Ben had started reading Matthew's Gospel to his mother. They had got to chapter eleven. Ben read out the last three verses.

"Come unto me, all ye that labour and are heavy laden, and I will give you rest. Take my yoke upon you, and learn of me; for I am meek and lowly in heart: and ye shall find rest unto your souls. For my yoke is easy, and my burden is light."

It was a bit hard for Ben to understand the old-fashioned language, but his mother explained that oxen were yoked together to plough in the fields. She had seen it in her childhood. They both realised that God was telling them that they didn't have to carry the burden of dad being "missing" alone. Jesus wanted to share it and give them peace and rest.

It was hard to continue normal life after that letter from the War Office. Ben and his mum dreaded the postman calling, but also longed to get good news. After a week they almost gave up hope that dad was alive. That was pretty well confirmed when a second letter arrived. This time it was from the officer who had been in charge of the special unit that had been mining tunnels under the German trenches. The letter said what a brave man Ben's dad was, and that having been missing for over a week, he was now listed as "missing, presumed dead". All the company were extremely sorry and sent condolences.

It was getting near the end of the school term and there were class exams. The last thing Ben felt like doing was studying. His mind kept drifting and his heart was heavy and sad. But he was determined to do well and made a massive effort to concentrate. He knew his dad had wanted him to go to grammar school and somehow he wanted to believe it would happen. Sometimes, though, he felt really down about everything. Perhaps his brothers would die in battle, or they would all go "missing, presumed dead", and he would have to go out to work to provide for his mum.

Ben's worries about his mum continued to grow as she became very thin as well as yellow. He begged her to stop work but she was determined to do her bit to fight this war, since it seemed the Germans had killed her husband.

The weather was very hot and every now and then there was a thunderstorm, but it didn't seem to clear the air. The hot weather made his mum even more tired. There was so much to do in the garden while the evenings were light, but they both struggled to get it done. Sometimes, Ben walked down to the Fleet and sat watching the sea birds. At least near the sea there was a bit more breeze. Most evenings he caught a rabbit for a stew, but his mum had little appetite now.

At the end of term the results were given out and Ben came top of the class, even beating Vera. "Your father would have been proud of you," the headmaster said, presenting Ben with a prize. It was a book called, *The Children of the New Forest*. He was thrilled to receive it, but hated that the headmaster had said “would have been proud”. In his heart Ben couldn’t accept his dad was dead and still prayed every night for him to be kept safe.

Chapter Fourteen

The Saturday after the exams were finished was the first chance that Ben, Sid and Vera had to try and find the spy's tunnel. Now that the day for detective work had finally arrived, the children were desperate to get going.

"If only it wasn't so hot, though!" complained Vera, fanning herself with a large leaf as they set off. It really was hot, without a breath of wind, just the occasional rumble of thunder.

"Why did you bother to come if you're just going to moan?" Sid retorted.

Ben wiped the sweat off his forehead. He tried to encourage them a bit. "Just think: soldiers have to walk in this heat all the time. And they have a heavy backpack to carry. I suppose that's why they sing as they march – to keep their spirits up."

"We could do that, too!" suggested Sid, and began a song which was popular that year to encourage the older men who had been conscripted into the army:

"Forty nine and in the army,
Forty nine – oh isn't it fine
Though I'm wheezy across the chest

And gouty about the knees,
I'm learning to shoulder arms
But I'd rather be standing at ease.
Forty nine and in the army
And soon I will be in the fighting line,
If somebody holds me rifle
While I borrow a pair of steps,
I'll be over the top and at 'em at forty nine!"

The others soon joined in, and it seemed to work – that and the peppermints Ben dished out, for without fail he still had his weekly pennyworth of peppermints in his pocket. They were still the Peppermint Detective Agency!

At the River Wey they stopped to watch the ducks. The water looked cool and inviting and they longed to paddle their hot feet, but they knew they had important work to do. Besides, more and more clouds were gathering now and if they didn't get a move on they'd be soaked!

St. Ann's churchyard was even more overgrown than the last time they had been there. The bees were humming and butterflies flitted around the flowers on the nettles. The moment had arrived. They crept quietly into the churchyard by the side of the school.

Ben's heart was thumping so loudly he thought the others might hear it. He didn't want his friends to know he was scared. This wasn't a game they were playing: this was for real! A spy might carry a gun and everyone had heard the rumour that Germans were ruthless and that they killed women and children. Then he remembered that he had prayed that morning asking Jesus to keep them safe, and he prayed again, quickly, under his breath.

"Where were you when you heard the grating sound, Ben?" asked Sid. Ben showed them where he had been standing, and they went to where he thought the noise had been coming from. They looked around for any clues.

For a while they couldn't see anything, but just as they were about to give up, Sid noticed that one stone in the wall somehow looked a bit different. It had a strange mark on it, which he thought was odd. He pressed it and it made the familiar grating sound. Ben gasped, and Vera clutched Sid's arm.

"You've found it!" she whispered. As she spoke, a flat slab near their feet opened up – and there was the tunnel! They peered cautiously down into the dark hole.

Ben had bought some matches from Mr. Savage's shop a few days ago and had them in his pocket. His hands were shaking as he lit one and held it near the entrance. Sure enough, as his eyes accustomed to the gloom, he saw a ledge with candles. He lit one and carefully let himself down into a cave very similar to the one in the church. Sid followed him.

"Shall I stay up here and stand guard?" suggested Vera. "If anyone comes, I could go and get help."

Sid nodded and Ben called up, "Good idea, Vera. If

there's any trouble, if the spy comes or something, just run over to the manor and get David."

"Try not to be too long," she said. "It'll be a bit boring here just waiting!"

"All right, back soon," said Sid, turning his attention to the cave.

"It looks like someone is living here!" said Ben in amazement, pointing out a black cape, a pair of trousers and a top hat, all laid carefully near the entrance.

A tunnel led from the cave, much like the one from the church. "Shall we explore it?" asked Sid, hopping from one foot to the other in excitement.

Ben nodded, and the boys cautiously made their way along the tunnel, the light of the candle casting eerie shadows on the walls. The stonework looked crumbly and very old, but sturdy. At various intervals there were narrow passageways leading off the main tunnel. They barely looked big enough for anyone to squeeze through. Perhaps they were some kind of drainage system, thought Ben. Or perhaps smugglers were much thinner in days gone by! In any case he didn't fancy going down any of them!

It was much cooler underground, but an unpleasant musty smell filled his nostrils and the air was heavy and damp. He was finding it hard to breathe and his legs felt tense and unnatural. A sudden scuttling sound caused him to gasp in fear. Then he realised it was just a mouse. Relief went through his body, so intense he almost felt like laughing.

Suddenly Ben stopped. The tunnel continued but to their right was another cave, like a tiny room.

"Hey, Sid, look at this!" whispered Ben. Sid peered over his shoulder. In the light of the candle, they could see a worn-out suitcase on a makeshift table. As they crept closer, they could see all sorts of letters, maps, diagrams and photos piled on top of the suitcase.

"What do you think this means?" asked Sid, poring over a piece of paper which had lots of crease marks on it as if it had been folded up very small and kept in a pocket or wallet. There was a random selection of letters and numbers on it.

"It looks like some sort of code!" said Ben. "And what about these?" he added, picking up a whole handful of photos. "That looks like Portland Harbour. And this one is definitely the torpedo works. I recognise the chimney."

They both looked at each other. Ben thought how odd Sid's face looked in the light of just one candle – older, more grown-up somehow and deadly serious. "Are you thinking what I'm thinking?" whispered Ben.

"Yes. This is it! The spy's hideout!"

Ben nodded. Somehow the awful reality of it hadn't really hit home until that moment. They were in enemy territory. And if the mole found them here, they were in big trouble. A distant echoing sound crashed in on their thoughts. The boys looked at each other in alarm.

"What was that? It sounded like the stone moving into place," said Ben, in a voice that didn't quite sound his own.

Sid's voice wavered. "Shall we go back and see or go on?"

"Go on, I think. It's probably just Vera, closing the stone because someone has come into the churchyard. We may not have another chance to explore."

Sid nodded, and the two boys went back to the main tunnel. It seemed to go on for ever. "Where do you think this leads?" asked Sid. Ben was just wondering if it went to the stable block, like the other tunnel, when they came to an abrupt end. If there had been an exit there it now seemed to have been bricked up.

"We'll that's it: we'll have to go back," said Ben. As he was turning round, the candle picked up another little cave.

"We must have walked past that without noticing," said Sid, indicating to Ben to bring the candle. Ben gasped in amazement.

"Oh my goodness!" said Sid. "This must be where the spy is living!" A bed was covered with a rough-looking blanket, and a box held tins of food and some other supplies.

"Let's get out of here," suggested Ben, turning to go.

Sid nodded. "Yes, we don't want to be caught here!" As they turned to go, the candle flickered and Sid caught sight of something glinting high up. "Look!" he whispered. "What's that?" Jutting out from the wall was a small ledge. On the ledge was a gun. Quickly, Sid shoved it down his pocket. "Just in case we get cornered," he explained to Ben. "You never know, it might be useful even if we don't know how to use it."

"Good idea," agreed Ben. "And it means the spy won't have a gun, if we've got it!" But even while Ben was still speaking, he heard the sound they least wanted to hear; footsteps, echoing along the tunnel they had just come through.

"Oh no!" whispered Ben. His mouth was dry and he felt rooted to the spot. A desperate glance around the cave confirmed there was nowhere to hide. The footsteps were getting closer and closer.

"We're trapped!" whispered Sid.

* * *

Outside, the weather had changed. Vera anxiously looked up at the sky as a band of heavy grey clouds covered the sun. Large drops of rain began to to fall. She hoped the boys wouldn't be too long down in the tunnel. She was getting more and more nervous just hanging around. A sudden clap of thunder made her jump out of her skin and then the rain really started.

She was just about to make a dash to shelter when she heard the gate creak at the entrance to the churchyard. Her heart thumping, Vera acted quickly. She pressed the stone to cover the entrance to the tunnel, and then clambered over the wall into the school playground. She crouched behind the wall and peeped through a gap in the stones, hardly daring to breath.

A man in a grey suit was pushing a bike towards the

tunnel entrance. He didn't appear to have seen Vera. He rested his bike against the wall and then pressed the stone to open the tunnel. Vera's heart skipped a beat. This was no ghost; this was the man who they had seen taking photos of the train! She had seen enough. The boys were in danger and she needed to get help!

Quickly and quietly, Vera skirted round the back of the school and headed for the manor house. She vaulted the railings at the edge of the playground, but her feet slipped as she landed and she fell. Gingerly, she lifted herself into a sitting position. Her hands stung. She moved to stand up and winced as pain shot through her right leg. It was bleeding from a gash. Her hair was dripping and her dress was fast getting wet in the rain. More thunder rolled overhead, followed by a flash of lightning. Vera ran like she had never run before.

Chapter Fifteen

"We've got to find somewhere to hide!" whispered Ben in a panic, hearing the footsteps coming closer.

Sid grabbed his arm. "Quick, we can hide in one of those narrow passages!" he hissed. He pulled his friend out of the cave and into a tight space round the back. Panic rose up inside Ben and his breathing quickened. He suddenly realised: The candle! The man would see the flame in the dark!

"Shall I blow it out?" he whispered to Sid. Sid nodded, and Ben blew it out. It was pitch black. Ben closed his eyes, so he could pretend it wasn't really that dark. He was glad of Sid's breathing next to him. The echoing footsteps came closer and closer, until Ben could make out the light of a lamp coming nearer and nearer. Suddenly he heard boots scuffle slightly at the entrance and walk in to the cave.

Ben had to open his eyes; he couldn't bear the suspense any longer, but to his surprise it wasn't so dark. Through a grating between them and the cave, at about head height, a light was shining! What a glorious chink of light! Ben grinned at Sid, who squeezed his arm. The boys silently sidled down the narrow passageway towards it, rather like moths attracted to light. Standing close together, they were both just tall enough to see through the grating. Standing with his back to them was a heavily-built man in a dark overcoat, carrying a suitcase. This was certainly no ghost!

* * *

It was really only a short distance to the Manor, but with her leg bleeding, and knowing the boys were in danger, it felt to Vera like miles. Eventually she reached the back door, breathless and sobbing. She banged on it hard, again and again.

As usual, Cook opened the door. "Goodness gracious, it's Vera, isn't it? Whatever's the matter?" she said, noticing the state of the girl. "Come in, child, come in."

Cook quickly grabbed a chair and plonked it in front of the stove. "I'll just put the kettle on, and then I'll get you a warm blanket and you can tell me all about it."

"No, no, it's Sid and Ben. Please help! I slipped and fell, but I'm all right, I just cut my leg I think. Sid and Ben are in trouble in a tunnel in the churchyard. I've come to get David and the police. It's a spy!"

"A spy?" asked Cook in astonishment. "In a tunnel in the churchyard? Are you sure?"

Vera nodded. "He's gone down the tunnel, after the boys. Please, we have to do something quickly!" Vera knew she wasn't making much sense, but Cook ran to the bell board in the kitchen and rang all the bells.

People came running from everywhere.

"Are we being invaded?" asked Molly, rushing through the kitchen door, closely followed by the gardener.

"I'm not sure. There's trouble though. Spies are here!" said Cook. "We need to send for the police at once!"

Just then, David walked through the door, followed by the butler. Vera quickly explained what had happened. Molly stood rooted to the spot, but David took command. He ran to fetch the shotgun they used for hunting game, sent the butler to fetch the police from Weymouth, and ran back to the kitchen.

"Come with me, bring the lantern," he called to the gardener. "We'll find the boys," he said. "Vera, you come and show me how to open the tunnel."

Vera ran to the door with David. Although in fact it had only been a few minutes since she had arrived at the manor, it seemed like ages and she felt sick with fear for Ben and her brother. What could ten-year-old boys do against a grown-up enemy spy?

* * *

The boys watched the spy fling the suitcase on to the bed. It was the same one they had seen earlier. The light, they now realised, was coming from a hurricane lamp, placed on the floor by the bed. The spy was rifling through the suitcase, clearly looking for something. He picked out what looked like a handful of photos and some pieces of paper, checked them against the light and hastily thrust them into his inside coat pocket.

Then something dreadful happened. Ben had been holding on to the wall with his hand, and suddenly a great chunk of it gave way. "Ow," yelled Sid, as the heavy stone landed on his foot. He quickly put his hand over his mouth, but it was too late.

The spy dashed out of the cave, with his lamp in his hand. "Who's there?" he called menacingly, in a foreign accent. "Come out, whoever you are!" The boys froze in terror. The spy didn't know where they were – yet. But he had a lamp. He didn't have his gun, but he was much bigger than them, and he could beat them up and lock them in the tunnel for ever, thought Ben.

Mesmerised and terrified, the boys nearly jumped out of their skin as the man shouted something foreign in the tunnel. The shout echoed all around the cave. "Come out, whoever you are!" he yelled again, this time in English. "You'll pay for interfering in business not your own! You don't stand a chance of escaping here alive, I'll see to that!" His voice was deep and he had a frightening foreign accent. "You'll never leave," he added with a sneer.

This terrible threat bounced around the walls of the tunnel. But at that moment Ben heard a quiet voice in his mind, "I will never, ever leave you." Suddenly he knew exactly what to do. Like David in the Bible story, he had his catapult and three smooth, round pebbles ready to catch rabbits.

Ben quietly passed the candle to Sid, crept down the passageway, put a stone into his catapult, and waited.

Sid followed him. He had his hand on the gun in his pocket, but was too scared to get it out. He was really glad the spy didn't have it, though!

The boys stood there in silence. Ben's heart was thumping so much he thought the spy would be able to hear it! There was silence for what seemed an eternity. Then the two boys heard the spy starting to walk out of the cave and move towards the passageway where they were hiding. His footsteps echoed ominously.

"Jesus, please help me," Ben prayed silently, as he readied his catapult. "Don't let me kill him like David killed Goliath, but please do something!" He pulled back on the catapult and let fire.

The stone hit the man on the knee. "Aagh!" he yelled, clutching his knee in agony. Ben took aim again, and this time hit the spy on the chin. For a moment there was a deadly silence. The spy held up his lamp. Ben's heart was thumping hard. Any minute now, the spy would see them! Nervously, Ben held his catapult ready. Just as the man turned he fired again.

For one awful second, Ben thought he'd missed. But no! He had hit the the spy in the temple. The man collapsed to the ground, his head in his hands, groaning in pain. The lamp flickered as it fell to the floor.

Just at that moment the boys heard footsteps and shouting: it was David! Arriving at the scene, he pointed the shotgun at the dazed spy, who suddenly looked very ordinary. Still groaning in pain he put his hands up.

By the time the police arrived, the man had been tied up with a length of rope that Ben had found in the cave, and everyone was breathing more freely. But it had been a close thing!

Chapter Sixteen

"Hold still, and smile please!" The camera flashed and the moment was captured. Sid, Ben, and Vera were all in their Sunday best, having their photo taken for the local paper, the Dorset Daily Echo.

The next day Ben rushed over to Mr. Savage's shop to get a copy of the paper, then dashed over to the twins' house. They all pored over it eagerly.

"Look at your face, Sid," laughed Vera in delight. "You look a proper gentleman!"

"You don't look bad, yourself," said Sid, with a grin.

Under the photo, was a report of the whole story: the bottle with the message, the secret tunnels, the Peppermint Detective Agency and even some background information about the spy. "It says here the authorities already knew quite a bit about the spy and were close to tracking him down. The spy knew he'd been rumbled and was about to make a quick getaway," said Ben.

"So that's why he was packing up all those papers and photographs," added Sid.

In the end, after he had been interrogated, it was discovered that the spy was the same man they had seen on the bike at Ferry Bridge. Even the gloves fitted him! He was also the "ghost" who had scared the choirboys. It had been his way of keeping people away from the churchyards, so that no one would discover his hiding place. The photos the children had seen in the spy's suitcase were all of important locations that would have been very useful to the Germans. They might even have helped them win the war!

"I was right about that photo of the torpedo works, then," said Sid, looking suddenly serious. "Our dad could have been blown up by the Germans if that spy had got back to Germany with all his information."

Captain Wray, the man who had written the original message, was given a special mention in the article for his bravery and ingenuity in composing the rhyme. A police sergeant went to see Captain Wray's wife. She had known for quite a long time that her husband had died at sea after a U-boat* attack. But she still cried when she saw her husband's handwriting and read the lovely things he'd written about her, and known how he had helped to catch the spy.

It had all been very exciting but, deep down, Ben was glad when everything began to return to normal. Whenever Ben remembered his ordeal in the tunnel, he reminded himself that God had kept his promise. He hadn't left him and he had answered his cry for help.

He enjoyed delivering for Mr. Savage and when the summer holidays came he helped his grandad from time to time in the lerret, catching mackerel. Most of the fish were sent by train to London, but sometimes Ben took fresh mackerel home for dinner, which was a delicious treat! Ben hoped it would make his mum get better, but it didn't seem to help.

Part way through the holidays a postcard arrived. Ben took it from the postman, thinking that it must be from Fred. As Ben turned it over, he realised that it had come from Germany, not France … it was from his dad! His Dad! It was amazing! His dad was alive!

There were just a few lines in his dad's neat handwriting. They said that he was in a prisoner of war camp in Germany. He was well, and loved them all very much. Ben read it quickly, then re-read it twice more. He could hardly believe it!

Everything was going to be all right! Ben ran round and round the garden, waving his arms in the air, and whooping with delight! His dad was alive! His dad was alive! His mum was at work, but he couldn't wait to tell her the good news. He ran to Chickerell and begged Mr. Savage to let him borrow the bike so that he could ride to the munitions factory to tell his mum. Mr. Savage was delighted with the news, and sent him off with a bag of peppermints!

The guard on the gate looked at the excited young lad, listened to his message and decided that everyone needed some good news. The war was making all the workers depressed, so he let Ben in and took him to the manager.

"This is good news!" the manager said, and blew a

whistle to made everyone stop work. All went quiet as the machines ground to a halt. "Mrs. Goodenough," he called. "There is some news good enough for you to go home for the rest of the day. Everyone else: back to work!" He laughed at his own joke, and then blew the whistle again.

Ben's mum took off her overalls and went into the office, quite mystified. When she saw Ben beaming all over his face, she somehow knew. "Is it your dad? Is he alive?" she asked, her face breaking into a wide smile.

Ben passed her the postcard."Yes, Mum, and he's not injured either. He's in a prisoner of war camp, but is alive and well, and sends his love to us all!"

Tears of joy ran down his mum's face. She hugged Ben so hard he could hardly breathe! She thanked the manager and then she and Ben walked home together. They went to tell the vicar and together the three of them gave thanks to God for the wonderful news.

"Mum," said Ben, as they came out of the vicarage, "I need to tell our Molly. She and David can then tell Albert. I'll go back to Mr. Savage and tell him where I'm going with the bike. I won't be long!"

As he cycled towards Radipole to spread the good news Ben found himself singing "Count your blessings, name them one by one" at the top of his voice. For the first time in weeks his heart felt light!

When he returned home, he and his mum celebrated together. Their appetites had miraculously returned and they really enjoyed a meal of fresh mackerel with a large mound of delicious fried potatoes!

That night Ben slept better than he had for a long time. However, he was woken in the early hours by the sound of a huge explosion. Ben began to shake. His first thought was that it was a Zeppelin raid. The sky was lit up, but it was from a fire, not the moon. Ben and his mum dressed quickly and ran up the lane, to where a crowd of people had gathered.

"The munitions factory has exploded," one man informed them.

"Dangerous thing, handling explosives," said another, shaking his head.

The next morning they found out that very few workers were in the factory on the night shift, and most of those had survived. Even so, it was horrible to know that some people had been killed. The factory itself was completely destroyed.

"Just think. It could have happened in the daytime when so many more people would have been at work," Ben's mum said in a bit of a daze.

Ben shuddered. His mum could have died, too. "Mum, I'm just glad you don't have to work there any more. Now you can get well!"

His mum nodded. "It's a bit of a relief to me too, I must confess. I've been feeling so unwell these past weeks. I'm sorry that I worried you so much. I think I will offer to help Sid and Vera's mum when the baby is born. Vera won't have to do so much then, so perhaps she can go back to school. I could also volunteer to help at the camp and look after the Australian soldiers when I get a bit stronger."

"That would be great, Mum! And with my wages at the shop, the rabbits I catch and Grandad's fishing, we will manage for money, won't we?"

His mum smiled, and fished in her pocket. "Of course we will. In fact," she continued with a smile, "here's a penny. Why don't you go and buy a pennyworth of peppermints and go winkling with Sid and Vera?"

Ben thought that was a great idea and ran off to Mr. Savage's shop, singing his "blessing song" as he went. Whatever happened, he knew that Jesus would always be with him.

Glossary

Chapter One

Farthings: At the time of the First World War, four farthings or two halfpennies (also called ha'pennies or a ha'pence) made one old penny. A threepenny coin was called a "thruppeny bit". Twelve pennies made a shilling, and twenty shillings made a pound.

Regiments: These were military units, consisting of several battalions, and were often linked to a county. They each had their own flag, to distinguish them from other units. These flags were called "colours".

Enlist: Men could "enlist" by volunteering to be in the armed forces. Later, men were forced to go if they were fit enough. This was called conscription.

White feather: "The Order of the White Feather" was formed in 1914. Women gave men who were not yet in the armed forces a white feather, as a sign of cowardice. It was very insulting, especially when given to men who would have liked to have gone to war but were not fit, too old or too young.

The First World War: The First World War (1914–1918) is sometimes known as "World War 1", "WW1" or "The Great War".

Scullery: This was the name for a room used for the storage of kitchen utensils and where some kitchen work was done, like preparing vegetables and washing up.

Larder: This was a large cupboard where food was stored. It was kept as cool as possible, away from the cooking range. There were no fridges or freezers in those days.

In service: Before World War 1, the only work many girls were able to do was to become servants in big houses.

Driftwood for the stove: Driftwood is wood washed up on shores and beaches. In the War it proved very valuable as firewood since it was free. Most people cooked on black range fires, fuelled by coal or wood. Coal, however, was scarce since it was needed for industry and trains.

Lerrets: A lerret was a small boat especially designed about three hundred years ago for use on Chesil beach, where there were steep banks of pebbles, surf and cross currents. The lerret was used to catch mackerel. Fishermen worked together in teams and shared the catch, but usually the lerret was owned by one person.

Chapter Two

Whitehead Torpedo Works: This was a very famous factory. It was named after a Mr. Whitehead, who invented the torpedo. Torpedoes were large, sausage-shaped weapons, which were launched from submarines or from small, fast war ships. They carried an explosive charge and were very effective in blowing up enemy ships.

Huns: This was a nickname used for the Germans in the First World War. It was quite a rude way of referring to them.

Food: During the First World War food became very scarce. The German submarines were blockading the British merchant navy ships that brought food into the country. The Germans wanted to starve the British people into surrender.

The Front Line: This was the place where the soldiers were engaged in fighting each other and the battle was actually happening.

Copperplate writing: This was a beautiful, elegant script which people were taught to use. The word came from engraving words on copper ready for printing. This neat writing showed the person had been well educated.

Chapter Three

Rabbit-hunting: This became necessary because there was so little meat.

Slate: Slates were used at school along with slate pencils before exercise books and pencils. The work would be rubbed out and the slate reused for years. Often children wore them around their necks on a string, to prevent them dropping them on the way to school and possibly breaking them.

Belgian Flush: Just before the war and then through the war years, everything associated with Germany and the Germans was hated, so German Measles became known as "Belgian Flush". German Shepherd dogs were renamed "Alsatians" and German music was not allowed to be played. Children were forbidden to play with German toys, and people with German backgrounds changed their names to more English-sounding ones.

Day-old bread, buns and cakes: these were often sold at half price and were a great treat for people who couldn't afford the full price.

Chapter Four

Workhouse: This was a public home for very poor people. Men, women and children were put into separate areas. They had to work very hard in return for their keep. It was like a prison and very degrading for people.

There was often a lot of cruelty and little care or understanding, so naturally, everyone was terrified of ending up there.

Consumption: Consumption was an old fashioned name for tuberculosis (TB). Before the development of antibiotics it was a much-dreaded disease, from which many patients did not recover.

Call-up papers: a summons to serve in the armed forces.

Reserved occupations: Men who were in "reserved occupations" were exempt from being conscripted. This was because they were doing other work considered essential for the war effort.

Trow: This was a small, flat bottomed rowing boat, which was used to row the lerret crew over the Fleet lagoon to the Chesil bank, where their boat was anchored. Often young boys would row the trow back over the Fleet, full of the mackerel caught by the lerret fishermen, and take them to Weymouth to be packed in ice and sent by train to London.

Chapter Six

Livery: A special uniform worn by a servant.

Chapter Seven

Winkling: Winkles are edible sea creatures that hide in seaweed and rock pools, and were a sought-after delicacy. Limpets are also sea creatures, slightly larger than winkles and with conical shells. They stick very tightly to the rocks and are difficult to prise off. They need to be kept fresh in a bucket of sea water. They were boiled for a few minutes and taken out of their shells and eaten with a little salt and vinegar.

Square Bashing: This is a nickname for the initial training given to a member of the armed forces, particularly soldiers. It involved a lot of drill and marching, learning to use weapons and what to expect in battle.

Chapter Eight

Women working: Until the First World War most wives and mothers stayed at home. There were no modern household appliances so all the chores took a long time and a lot of hard work.

Chapter Nine

Raddle man: He was called by different names in different parts of the country. In Dorset it was raddle, in other places, reddle and ruddle. All these words mean 'red'.

Chapter Ten

Sexton: This was a person who took care of the church building and everything inside it. He often also acted as grave digger and took care of the churchyard.

Chapter Eleven

V.A.D.: Stands for "Voluntary Aid Detachments". Many women's groups started during the First World War. Since so many men had gone to fight, it gave opportunities for women to help in lots of ways. The Voluntary Aid Detachments had many young women in their ranks who helped to care for the wounded troops, as there were not enough trained nurses. After the war, many trained to become fully-qualified nurses.

The Allies: This was a term for the group of countries who joined together to fight against Germany.

Chapter Twelve

Milk trains: These ran throughout the country in the early hours of the morning, picking up the milk that farmers had brought to the stations in large churns and taking them to the large cities to be sold.

Toilets: Toilets at home were outside in a separate building in the garden.

Cockney: This is a term used to describe a Londoner born within the sound of Bow Bells. Now it is widely used to denote anyone born in central London. These people, particularly those living in the East End, and costermongers who worked in the markets, had their own rhyming slang and way of speaking.

Private: This was the name for a newly-enlisted soldier.

Zeppelin: This was the name of the German airships that terrorised England, particularly London. They dropped bombs that caused much damage and loss of life. They were not very accurate and sometimes got blown off course, so there was accidental damage even if the intended targets were not always destroyed. After Lieutenant Robinson shot down a Zeppelin, his technique was used by other pilots and several were destroyed and the raids decreased.

Bobby shop: This was a nickname for the police station.

Shooting Zeppelin airships down: In September 1916, a Lieutenant Robinson did manage to shoot down an airship and was awarded a Victoria Cross for his bravery.

Chapter Thirteen

U-boat: This was the term for a German submarine.

Recipes

War Bake

This is the kind of food many poor people had to eat. Does it sound appetising to you?

1lb (450g) Minced bacon fat
Stale bread
Leftover vegetables
Two tablespoonfuls of oats
1 pint of water

Mix all the ingredients together and pour into a baking dish. Bake in a moderate oven for 30 minutes at 340-370°F (170-185°C) Gas Mark 4. Turn out and eat cold with pickles or brown sauce.

Genuine Portland Dough Cake

This recipe has been handed down through my family for at least four generations. Mrs. Smith at Radipole Bakery would have used it! I think you would like this. Get your mum or dad to try it!

1lb of bread dough (450g) weighed out after the first proving.
8oz fat. (225g) White fat is best
8oz dried fruit (225g)

6oz sugar (175g)
½ teaspoon nutmeg
¼ teaspoon mixed spice

Knead the sugar and fat very well into the dough until quite sticky. Add the fruit and spices. If too sticky to handle, add a little dry flour.

Place in a tin and allow to rise in a warm place for about 15 minutes.

Place in oven for about 1 hour at 360°F (180°C) Gas Mark 4.

Enjoy!